PENGUIN BOOKS

WRITERS FROM THE OTHE
General Editor: Philip Roth

THE CITY BUILDER

George Konrád, born in Hungary in 1933, studied literature at the University of Budapest. He worked as a social worker, editor, and sociologist, publishing a number of essays on both literature and sociology. His first novel, *The Case Worker* (available in Penguin), was translated into many languages and brought him worldwide recognition. Konrád's other works include *The Intellectuals on the Road to Class Power* (written with Ivan Szelényi), and, most recently, the highly acclaimed novel *The Loser*.

George Konrád lives in Budapest.

GEORGE KONRÁD

THE CITY

*Translated from the Hungarian by
Ivan Sanders*

*Introduction by
Carlos Fuentes*

PENGUIN BOOKS

BUILDER

PENGUIN BOOKS

Viking Penguin Inc., 40 West 23rd Street,
New York, New York 10010, U.S.A.
Penguin Books Ltd, 27 Wrights Lane, London W8 5TZ
(Publishing & Editorial) and Harmondsworth, Middlesex,
England (Distribution & Warehouse)
Penguin Books Australia Ltd, Ringwood,
Victoria, Australia
Penguin Books Canada Limited, 2801 John Street,
Markham, Ontario, Canada L3R 1B4
Penguin Books (N.Z.) Ltd, 182–190 Wairau Road,
Auckland 10, New Zealand

First published in the United States of America by
Harcourt Brace Jovanovich, Inc., 1977
This edition with an introduction by Carlos Fuentes published in
Penguin Books 1987
Published simultaneously in Canada

LIBRARY OF CONGRESS CATALOGING IN PUBLICATION DATA
Konrád, György.
  The city builder.
  (Writers from the other Europe)
  Translation of: A városalapító.
  I. Title. II. Series.
PH3281.K7558V313 1987   894'.511'33   87-11953
ISBN 0 14 00.9947 6

Printed in the United States of America by
R. R. Donnelley & Sons Company, Harrisonburg, Virginia
Set in Electra

In one of his splendid lectures on military history, Oxford professor Sir Michael Howard recently defined war for a Cambridge audience as "the careful management of violence." Howard is eminently aware of the lackluster shields of modern warfare; technology has destroyed the attractiveness of war as a way of life: no more knights in shining armor. Technology, as Max Weber put it, has disenchanted the world. And instead of the careful management of violence in battlefield-as-tournament, we have the careless unleashing of violence on civilian populations. Picasso's *Guernica* and Hersey's *Hiroshima*, as well as a thousand photos and film clips from Coventry, London, Nagasaki, and Dresden, have made us all aware of this in my generation.

INTRODUCTION:
THE CITY AT WAR

In *The City Builder*, the Hungarian novelist George Konrád zeroes in on one of the uglier aspects of modern warfare, which is the daily, insidious, silent, undeclared war of city planners against city dwellers: the war of the manipulators of life against the livers of life; the violence of those who by planning our happiness ensure our unhappiness, pitted against the response of those who try to live daily life in spite of unhappiness, and achieve their purpose through a string of minimal acts of love, sensuality, humor, creativity, and friendship. It is no novelty; it has always been so. But the *consciousness* of the fact has changed. This, again, has always been so: our times are what we make of them, directly through experience or indirectly through imagination. No matter what our sympathy for the Greek *polis* or the Florentine city state, we cannot have a consciousness of the problems that we might share with them except in terms of our own difficulties.

George Konrád is a Hungarian. He is a Central European. He is not alien to any of the cultural or political pressures of this emplacement, and his essays in *Antipolitics* contain some of the most lucid statements ever written about things such as living on the Eastern side of the Iron Curtain while remaining centrally situated in the culture of Middle Europe, this kingdom of the spirit, as Milan Kundera has seen it. I shall come back to this. But, straight off, I want to remind the readers of *The City Builder* that Konrád's theme and style go well beyond any variant of violence, coexistence, solidarity, or planning Utopia while living Topia. The prurient warrior looking here for a novel about totalitarianism should best look elsewhere; Kundera has memorably said that totalitarianism does not deserve the honor of a novel; but, Konrád is implicitly telling us, the city dweller does deserve it. The civil society *merits* a novel, because a novel is part of living, of dwelling in the city, and of making the city human. Again, Konrád does not shy away from the situation that he is in, and he can characterize it as harshly as any of us who, naively, believe that we truly live in "the free world." "The philosophy of dictatorship applies the laws of the war of people against people to the coexistence of individuals," he writes in *Antipolitics*, and, dramatizing this extreme reality in *The City Builder*, he also magnifies it: "I belong to a generation of murderers . . . who in order to avoid being killed became killers themselves . . ." But then he universalizes what he has first rendered particular and then dramatic: "I don't want a city . . . where if I love one human being I cannot love another and my body, if it desires another body, must feign shame . . ."

The third quote from *The City Builder* could have been uttered by an inhabitant of Counter Reformation Madrid or colonial Mexico City, of Puritan Boston or Victorian London, not only of Communist Budapest. Let us keep in mind this dramatic universality which is part of Konrád's greatness as a writer, as we remember quote number one—the dictatorship applying the laws of war to the life of the city and its people— and quote number two—the victims becoming killers to avoid being killed: we are dealing not only with a critical novel but with an oracular narrative, in which the grandeur and servitude of living in the *polis* (living *politically*) should be seen in poetic and prophetic terms, almost in the way that Walter Benjamin's Angelus Novus finally stands still, spreads his wings, and looks back on the ironical perfection of history: the Angel's rumination on the past redeems the city by seeing it as a ruin; and being a ruin means that it has survived and can show us its bare bones; its ruin is its eternity and thus its perfection. I guess that a Mexican and a Hungarian, a Latin American and a Central European, can share this vision and understand it: Latin America's greatest contrast with Anglo America is our experience of defeat while living side by side with the North American success story. Perhaps nothing shocks us and blinds us to mutual understanding as much as this. The United States will not accept defeat; its whole history is premised on happiness and success; the United States was promised success and feels sick and disoriented when it is handed defeat. Latin America shares Central Europe's familiarity with defeat, as defined by Konrád in *Antipolitics*: "Our defeats are milestones on the road to Eastern European liberation . . . Catastrophes are its schoolbooks . . . On a winding road there is a greater likelihood of accidents." When Konrád writes that "There is no total defeat," he is not only illuminating his own novels, but ours in Latin America as well. But are we both, Central Europeans and Latin Americans, not echoing the great tragic voice of the greatest North American novelist of our century, William Faulkner, who in the midst of self-congratulatory success could remind his society that happiness, the exceptional, could not define our humanity as certainly as unhappiness, the experience shared by the majority of human beings? Between pain and nothingness, Faulkner would choose pain. It is the choice of "the unvanquished."

George Konrád is not an apocalyptical novelist; he is an oracular one. He does not propose a Doomsday vision of his own city: "We who live in Budapest—right between East and West"—do not live in the worst of all possible worlds: "Budapest isn't a bad place to think in. Without a little danger, thinking loses its edge." But, he adds wryly, "too much danger isn't to be recommended." He does not mince words when he speaks of the real and enormous dangers suffered by Hungary along with Central Europe: all of the spontaneously emerging desires of Central Europe (neutrality, a multiparty system, self-government within the structure of the Soviet empire) are compatible in logical reality but incompatible in political reality: Soviet military retaliation has followed each time that a peripheral country has tried to free itself from any essential feature of the Soviet model. Loyalty to the Soviet Union and loyalty to the Communist Party remain the dictatorial conditions of the system.

The difficulties for the city and the citizen are thus immense; Konrád does not sweep them under the rug as he argues (again in consonance with most Latin Americans) for a multipolar world beyond the bipolar condominium of Yalta politics. But precisely because the difficulties are enormous, the search for exceptions becomes excitingly creative. Konrád, in his essays, offers a full panoply of avenues for acting within the system in order to melt it down. The difficulties are there, and they signify that it is impossible to democratize society by trying to overthrow the national Communist elite. Konrád offers the example of Southern Europe—Portugal, France, Greece—where the process of democratization was not revolutionary. The political elites of Salazar, Franco, and the Greek colonels were not overthrown. They were absorbed by the rapidly expanding middle class and the technocracy. And while it might be judged disingenuous to compare the fate of three Mediterranean nations within the renounceable NATO alliance to the nations of Central Europe caught in the webs of the Warsaw Pact, Konrád has a longer view on the matter, and it comes from within the Communist society, where the old recipe was that a regime is overthrown by mass movements. The new recipe, argues Konrád, is the transformation of the political structure by means of slowly ripening social transformations. It is a democratic vision, in which political changes are preceded by social changes. It is a humanistic vision, in the best sense of the word: "By definition, society is self-shaping and experimental, since it is made up of individual human beings with wills of their own. All existing rules are human . . . They are our work, and if we don't like them, we can make others instead . . ." This humanistic approach is that of Gianbattista Vico, the Neapolitan creator of modern historiography who first saw history as our own creation and responsibility in 1744. It meets one of its greatest challenges in contemporary Marxist-Leninist regimes, which believe that they are the dogmatic incarnation of the rules of history. Konrád is aware of this and that is why he searches so avidly and against such odds, for humanistic and historical, social, cultural, and individual contexts to support his "meltdown" vision of the Communist state.

Irony is one of his principal arms in this search. He reminds us of the fact that Hungarian cities, under the Dual Monarchy, were more noble and military than bourgeois, and that the bourgeoisie itself was more German and Jewish than Hungarian; the country was basically a nation of peasants, their culture intact, their numbers a majority: the villages were more populous than the cities. After World War II, it was, ironically, the Communist leadership that unleashed the impetus toward a bourgeois society in Hungary, something that neither the Communists nor their adversaries expected. This was achieved in close relationship to the demands of Hungarian nationalism: "For a thousand years, the Hungarian state was able to function with relative autonomy . . . at once the defender and the oppressor of its people." A Mexican descendant of the Virgin of Guadalupe and the liberal Benito Juárez, now living under the uninterrupted rule of the Party of Revolutionary Institutions (PRI), can eerily identify with these words, as well as with the following: "Throughout Hungarian history, our main aspiration has been a Hungarian state . . . We may get angry at our state and consider it unjust, but we want it to exist . . ."

The supreme irony of this situation in Hungary, as we all know, is that the man (and the system) employed by the Soviets to repress the 1956 uprising turned out to be, in the final analysis, the man (Kadar) and the system (so-called "gulash communism") that preserved a minimum of independence for Hungary, its state, the nation, the society, and its intellectuals.

Indeed, ironies abound and the writer, the prince of the ironical, does not miss a single one of them: On their greatest national holiday, Hungarians walk to the statue of a poet, Sandor Petöffi, on the day when he printed a poem without permission from the censor. The two fetishes of Hungarian existence may be loyalty to the Soviet alliance and to Communist Party rule; imagine the "sense of triumph" of the writer when he succeeds, explains Konrád, in "avoiding this pair of taboos." The avoidance can be elevated to an aesthetic. "Our censors envy us," he states in another page of *Antipolitics*. "They too would like to say what they think. I am an optimist because I know that desire is bolder than fear."

George Konrád lives in a society where there are limits to openness and limits to freedom. He is wary of saying that this is equivalent, in present-day Hungary, to tight totalitarian control, and fears that "people who call the government totalitarian" are looking for "an excuse for their own cautious accommodation to censorship." For similar, although paradoxical, reasons, he is wary of the theatrical intrusion of the foreign media in Hungarian affairs: "It is not in our interest to have a legion of correspondents busy sharpening our differences . . . If there is too much press attention on us, we will wind up talking not to the issues . . . but to an international audience hungry for sensation." Konrád is hard and sharp-eyed when he reflects that "international public opinion's approval and disapproval alike are transient things, a matter of fashion." Not that he does not applaud the international media's role as "auxiliaries" in the Hungarian national enterprise. He is simply aware of a rarely articulated resemblance between the modern media and modern uses of power: both are willing to see in independent words a crime and present them as a theatrical provocation.

Nothing could be farther from George Konrád's brand of optimism: desire is bolder than fear. This knowledge has a firm foundation. Its name is civil society. This is a term that has tremendous resonance in Central Europe, in Latin America, and in Mediterranean Europe, while it is pale or misunderstood in the democratic Anglo-American tradition. The reason is evident: for the English and the North American, civil society is something not mentioned because it is taken for granted. The United States, the only great nation of the twentieth century without a medieval heritage, sees itself born from an act of reason and a pure will to freedom in 1776: it is both the Minerva, fully armed, and the Venus, divinely born, of the modern world. The conflicts between church and state, pluralism and monism in politics, vertical and horizontal structure of authority, dogmatism and a united, hegemonical language, simply were not there, whereas they were very much alive in Hungary, in Mexico, or in Italy, where Antonio Gramsci best and most opportunely reminded us that civil society is all that cannot be absorbed by the structures and powers of official institutions.

Church, army, and state, for example, are the oldest and most monopolistic institutions of power in Latin America, where very little has ever been left outside of them, political reality being defined mostly by the interactions and relative strengths of bureaucrats, clergy, and officers, with exceptional eruptions of popular revolt. Gramsci warned that Russia was dangerously unsuited for socialism precisely because of the lack of a civil society in a country dominated not only by church and state, but by the perfect agreement between the two. The values entertained by both Dostoevsky and Solzhenitsyn—Caesaropapism or the monism of church and state, of religious and political authority—were simply secularized by the Russian Communist state: Marxism as quasi-religious dogma is inseparable from the state, its incarnation and executor. The distance, disorganization (and occasional madness) of the Spanish Empire, *defensor fides* and bulwark of the Counter Reformation, made such unity of purpose and closeness of vision more difficult to sustain in colonial Spanish America. But building civil societies has been a challenging task in Mexico, Peru, Argentina, Guatemala, El Salvador, or Nicaragua, where the political heritage of Saints Augustine and Thomas—monistic unity in order to achieve the common good, distrust of pluralism—have not sponsored the expansion of the civil society. Writers have been, in Russia, in Poland, in Czechoslovakia, in Hungary, in Mexico, in Argentina, in Cuba, in Chile, the great upholders of the fragile margin we call "the civil society."

As we recognize ourselves, with all the imaginable historical variants, in Central Europe's intense search for the foundations of the civil society beyond the Soviet imperative and the Communist monism, we find that George Konrád's ideas are indeed relevant to many societies in today's world. But the uniformity with which most people in the West, headed by the sensationalist media and certain simplistic heads of state, deal with the developments within Central Europe, leads to a brittle Manicheism: the West is good and free, the East is bad and enslaved, critics of the system in the East are freedom fighters, we should help them revolt, pity them, patronize them and wish they were here with us in this anchor's booth, this academic pulpit, this cozy op-ed corner. There is an almost smug, self-congratulatory belief that what a Central European wants to be is, quite simply, a Happy Gringo. Konrád is trenchant about this: The United States, he writes, should cease to be obsessed with its lecture-platform self-congratulation as the strongest, richest, freest, noblest, most unselfish nation, overreacting neurotically to every setback and every challenge, seeing intrigue, ingratitude, and Communist machinations wherever other people, having interests that don't coincide with the U.S.A.'s, insist on pursuing them anyway. Konrád recalls the famous phrase by the Hungarian Communist Party boss Matyas Rakosi: "Comrades, have we sunk so low as to be taken in by our own propaganda?" Sometimes, reading the so-called neoconservatives (who are neither new nor conservative, but middle-aged and either lapsed Trotskyites or Fascists who dare not say their names) in the North American press, I wonder if they too have not sunk to the belief in their own propaganda.

They certainly remind us just how different it is to commiserate with "Eastern" Europe, condemning it to its misery by dismissing reform in the Soviet Union as a sham (which it might well be) while willfully forgetting that, on our own purely humanistic and democratic terms, Soviet society is not doomed, as Germany or Japan were not, to historical embalmment. Are we, or are we not, all a part of the "self-shaping and experimental" world, as the work of man, that Konrád speaks of? Well before *glasnost* and the appearance of Mikhail Gorbachev, George Konrád was writing that

> We have the most fundamental interest in Soviet reform. We cannot create a life truly worthy of human beings for ourselves so long as our neighbors do not undertake to create the same for themselves. With a reformist Soviet Union, we could reinterpret our relationship with more detachment, refining it into genuine friendship.

At the time of writing this, Konrád lamented that "Moscow has not carried out its own reform," since "reformist allies" (in Budapest, in Prague, in Warsaw . . .) "could deal more easily with a reformist Soviet leadership." Konrád's prophetic words will soon be put to the test. If we believe in the concrete life of the city dwellers, in Russia as well as in Central Europe, we will wish them well as they reshape their societies. If we believe in the superiority of city planners in the West, we will hope that city planners in the East fail, since, as the Machiavellis of the airwaves put it in the United States, it is not in the interest of the West that things should go well in the Soviet Union or its satellites. They should go badly.

Konrád reminds us that the development of Central European societies leads to something that the present systems in Washington or Moscow are certainly uncomfortable with and that is the union of political democracy with economic democracy. In Soviet-dominated societies, there is neither. But in the capitalist democracies, Konrád warns us, while politics is liberal and democratic, the economy is hierarchically organized and directed from the top down, responding to the decisions of the owners. Konrád bids us imagine something else: a post-Communist and post-capitalist society. Central

Europe cannot simply turn back, given its development within state capitalism, with its concomitant creation of an ironical middle class benefiting from welfare structures, to pre-Communist conditions. It must go beyond them. In 1956, in 1968, and in 1980, Hungarians, Czechs, and Poles tried to create a society for themselves, beyond capitalism and beyond Communism. They were repelled each time and probably will be repelled again. But their reasons should not be confused with some kind of nostalgia for becoming the South Koreas or Singapores of Central Europe. The strength and persistence of their social and political action stems from their originality: beyond capitalism, beyond Communism, the movements in Central Europe propose civil societies where the different social groups can communicate freely with one another and govern themselves with less and less intrusion from the central state. The key concept, for Konrád and many others beyond the Iron Curtain, is self-management, meaning that "representative democracy spreads from the political sphere to the economic and cultural spheres as well." In *Antipolitics* he adds: "It means that democracy is the prevailing principle of legitimacy in the factory, in the research institute, in every institution—not party rule or corporate rule." Self-management poses, for Konrád, "the question of questions": should property belong to the state or the society? The response is called Solidarity, and it is a response that cannot be liked by either party or executive board. The sympathy of Western politicians for Lech Walesa and the social movement in Poland, argues Konrád, was meant to annoy the Soviet politbu008o. They really didn't care for a movement that radically undermined the power monopoly of every political class, while including virtually all of society.

Now, it seems that Solidarity, the very emblem of Central Europe's struggle for the civil society, is defeated. But we know what Konrád and others like him think of these "milestones on the road . . . to liberation," of these catastrophic "schoolbooks." Solidarity "is waiting; it is not storming the public squares, but it is at home in every dwelling."

This latest statement brings us to the heart of the Central European idea of the civil society and to the threshold of George Konrád's augural, universal novels of human predicament as city dwellers. The goal is not the reform of the party state but the creation of a civil society that cannot be defeated by the party state—a civil society that can melt down "the iceberg of power." When? All the time, starting now. How? Konrád believes that "the most effective way to influence policy" is to change a society's customary thinking patterns and "tacit compacts." Granted: "State society can be created quickly, but civil society takes a long time to build." Granted: the state has hegemony over society, it possesses nuclear forces, it consents to an alliance that can take the country into nuclear war. But, clearly, such power is power over something: it is power over people. Another Central European, Joseph Conrad, imagined, fearfully, a power over nothing, and this power is akin to madness: Kurtz in the heart of darkness. In Aztec Mexico, the emperor Moctezuma, on learning from the oracles that people were dreaming about the fall of the empire, had the dreamers rounded up in his palace, there to retell their dreams and then to be slaughtered. Moctezuma believed that if the dreamers were killed, the dreams would die. Only total extermination can assure total power, but then power is worthless.

The civil society. When, how, where? Humbly, minutely, "withdrawn, hunkered down in their mouseholes," aware of the dangers and gigantic obstacles, willing to wait one or two generations in socializing the system, with no desire to bring down governments because "we do not want to be government leaders" but rather people who do and go on doing what they like to do, "loyal to Montaigne and Spinoza, Goethe and Tolstoy—not to a mere head of state or party secretary." The success of a growing, independent civil society in Central Europe is not measured by the replacement of one government by another, but by the fact that, under the same government, the society gains strength, independent people multiply, the network of conversations that cannot be controlled from above becomes more dense:

> Our real mood is one of neither victory nor defeat, but of experimentation. When I look around I see that everyone is starting something, planning, trying his skills, telling of some small success. It may be an experimental school, an interesting research project, a new orchestra, a publishing opportunity, a screenplay accepted, a little restaurant about to open, an association of mathematicians, an attractive private shop, a private gallery, a trip to the West, cultural undertakings, independent publications, semi-underground journals . . .

A second culture is coming into being: "Hungarian society is beginning to resemble us," writes Konrád. His novels are an essential part of this minute, humble, generational, probing democratic activity which can only occur from within—"Clearly, the democracy that exists where I am means more to me than the democracy that exists someplace where I am not." Born from this depth, the novels of George Konrád can then achieve a universal resonance: they speak for all of us, not only for Hungary, or Central Europe, or the Soviet sphere, but for all that we share as humanity with them, making ourselves a part of the satanized Other, the Evil Empire indeed, the reliable villain without which the public, the media, and the authorities of the West cannot sleep in peace. Konrád not only permits us to see these complex realities from within, he projects them outside himself, outside of Hungary, as conflicts of human existence: oracular fictions which are ours as much as they are Hungarian and Central European.

The city planner plans for the city dweller's benefit, instead of letting him live and grow freely. What are the city planner's rules? He exchanges the power of money for the power of the edict. He unites dialectics and Utopia: ". . . they are no longer an ethical alternative but reality's aspiration, incorporated in the structure of the state." He aims at a joint possession of knowledge and might. Like Kurtz and Moctezuma, the city planner would like to reign over Everything, which is like reigning over Nothing: "Absolute power is the complete absence of power; by turning random events into law, we anoint chance as our king." The city planner believes that he has ceased to be a dreamer, because he is now backed up by computers. In reality, he has delivered us all to the reign of chance, and so "the danger now resides in us, in our careless and violent structures." The city dweller faces the city planner and begs for a communion of sorts, the communion of self-criticism for both planners and dwellers. This is a novel about the painful passage from city planner to city dweller.

Instead of the city planned, the dweller wants a city lived; he thus creates his own Utopia: "I wanted to cut through this resisting structure . . . and build a new city in its place." The dweller's Utopia is an Anti-Utopia to the planners, it is a city "not only thought of but also thinking itself." But it is also a voluntary, not a natural, city: "I want a left-wing city, a destructively constructive, diffusely coherent dialogue about the perils of being human . . ." Among those perils, there is the danger of Utopia itself. Few concepts of the humanistic universe are as controversial. Ancient peoples imagined Utopia in the past: Utopia was the founding city, the capital of the Golden Age, as recalled by both Ovid and Don Quixote. Utopianism was an exercise in mythical imagination. The Christian world, fleeing from a fallen nature, set Utopia in the future, and the industrial world secularized futurization: Utopia will happen in the future time but in the present space: here, but later. The humor of this eighteenth-century idea is illustrated by a character in a play by Goethe who decides to substitute natural flora with a metal garden, or by Uncle Toby

Shandy and his Sergeant Trim re-creating the battlefields of the War of the Spanish Succession in the cabbage patch of Shandy Hall. The crime and terror of radical Utopianism— the "final solutions"—are to be seen in Hitler's Reich and Stalin's Gulag: the city of the sun as a crematorium ringed by barbed wire. But the humanity and wisdom of the Utopian desire are to be found, also, in Thomas More's vision of a society open to constant renewal because the community is constantly changing and demanding new forms from individuals and state alike, constantly leaving open the question of political organization. Utopia happened, fleetingly, in the New World, when men such as Father Vasco de Quiroga created Utopian communities in Mexico, based on More's teaching, to protect the Indian population.

In between the Utopia of the planner and the Utopia of the dweller, Konrád's novel places four contending and throbbing realities: nature and sensuality, death and solidarity. There is no reflection on Utopia—the City Planned—that is not a reflection on nature: Why should we build a city when we have nature? Well, Konrád responds, we no longer have nature. We have exploited it to survive.

> We are no longer protected by nature's vast properties; when we make a move we confront one another, not nature. What was formerly self-regulated has become the task of planners.

Yet nature asserts itself, intrudes between our confrontations, reminds us of what we have killed in order to be: nature is the name of our lost innocence. This subjection to the same matter that we exploit is wonderfully rendered, time and again, by George Konrád in this novel. Catastrophically, nature floods a village; a wolf cub shakes its fur on a drifting roof, ducks swim, sows "sway in the water, their teats turned toward the sky"; a fox chases a pheasant cock; yesterday's plowland turns grey; today's is blacker; pikes of apples look like gabled roofs.

But the disaster of nature is saved by its own stubborn beauty and sensuality.

Here is Konrád describing the flight of the seagulls:

> Air itself defined their firm tail-feathers, the arch of their bones, their bulletlike heads. They are indifferent jewels on a perfect sky, and their flight is a flawless festival and hunt . . .

Their beauty and freedom are not ours:

> They want neither to solidify nor to change things. They fly over absences and over the repulsive alliance of virtue and vice. They don't differentiate between their nourishment and themselves.

We do: we are guilty. They are innocent of any relationship with us, even as they feed us, except the relationship of death. Our sensuality is not natural, it is a compensation of the death we inflict on nature and an exorcism against the death which awaits us. It is an intermission: our joy, our bane:

> The one without whom I couldn't sleep, whose thigh I had to touch in trains and parks, who had more fragrance behind her ear than a flower stall, whom I lifted high many a time and who shrieked with joy, whose every flaw I blandly forgave— why did I torment her while she was alive?

Konrád's response to the murder of natural life by human life, to the compensation of nature by sensuality, to the unnatural planing of the city, and to the city dweller's own impossible Utopia, is the title of a movement we have often mentioned, a politics, yes, and an antipolitics too, a universal reality that, nevertheless, the writers of Central and Eastern Europe have touched upon with greater sureness than any: Solidarity is the name of our only possible, human, saving activity and response to nature, power, death, and the city planned, while on earth: Solidarity is the city lived, the city built by those who live it.

Konrád was a social worker in Hungary and, in the novel of that title, *The Case Worker*, he gives us one of the most moving narratives of concrete solidarity since Dostoevsky. The Case Worker sees at close quarters the horror of the city, the city at war, and the protagonist of the city strife is an idiot child whom no one wants and who the Case Worker will take if he is to save himself and give some matter to his beliefs in Solidarity as the response of the city dweller to the city planner: not another Utopia, but the concreteness of caring for a living creature and taking that creature on as *my responsibility*.

The horror of the city is the horror of the child in *The Case Worker*: "this brainless child, from whom nature has withheld even the knowledge of fear." Orphaned, abandoned, described in the most precise manner, his acts not bordering on, but wallowing in, putrefaction, the idiot child is wholly dependent on the care of the Case Worker. Yet it is he, the Case Worker, who is trapped by the child and becomes dependent on him. "A ghost with flesh," the child poses a nagging, profound question for his carer's life: for what purpose was this idiot devised? And, most culpably, he tempts the Case Worker: to wash "this abstract object, to scrub down his cage and hand him a piece of horsemeat, to give him milk, put salve on his scabrous skin . . . massage his swollen belly, tickle the back of his neck, push his tongue back behind his teeth . . ." All of these caring motions cannot, finally, obscure the terrible fact that "idiots are the blood relatives of inanimate objects," that they have renounced memory, and that if the Case Worker left the room, the idiot would forget him forever. The idiot is our responsibility yet we depend totally on him: he remembers us only if we are present, which is no memory whatsoever; he makes us confront the terrible democracy of nature, he is "the hero of the here and now, foster brother of objects, our masters."

The image of the idiot child crowns Konrád's immensely moving narrative preoccupations about our place in the world: The idiot "is a born democrat who does not deprive objects of the freedom that must someday be restored to them willy-nilly." The circle would be closed if it were not for the failed exorcism of death. We have killed nature, we shall be killed by nature. The murderers are murdered: Georges Bataille, the twentieth-century French writer, reminds us that original peoples saw in death an assassination.

The solidarity of death gives forth a piercing, ironical cry in Konrád: Do not kill yourselves; that is far too original; let us do the job for you. Are we left with death and bureaucracy as our only concrete realities, death regulated by bureaucracy, bureaucracy nourished by death, yet another circle twining itself around our possibilities, hampering them forever?

In *The City Builder,* George Konrád gives a meaning and an expression to death that is both an acceptance of its inevitability and a redemption of life's continuity. The narrator of the novel lives through one of man's most painful experiences: the death of the father. Not that women are not equal sufferers; perhaps they are simply and rightfully different. Father and son: the Wordsworthian inversion, the child is the father of the man, becomes in Konrád an almost mythical echo of Father and Son as noncontemporaneous twins, sharers of the same belly that they have fecundated and been fecundated by.

The father dies. The child is taken away. The crippled city becomes the city dweller's charge: in the name of the father, in the name of the swallow, in the name of the rubbish, in the name of the child, the city planner has become the city dweller.

The oracular nature of this beautiful novel, its universal appeal, is summed up in these words:

Let him go before he sets fire to his father's house. The city wants to remain and the boy wants to go. If he is made to stay, he will dream of earthquakes.

The precision and beauty of George Konrád's language, let me finally say, is not the least of the arms he employs for his constructive criticism of the city of mankind. Konrád gives back the words to the tribe: I receive them in Mexico as his readers receive them in Budapest or New York City. They are powerful words since, as the French philosopher Alain put it, justice does not exist only in words, but first of all it exists in words. We shall know, one day, whether the words were stronger than the silence they opposed. Or rather, we will not know. The society of men and women will exist because it received and repeated and loved these words and, created by them, it went on to create further languages. Kundera has written that the history of the novel is the history of its continuity. In Konrád, this tradition appears incarnate in the life of the society. *The City Builder* is a novel that bears its own epigraph hidden somewhere in its heart: *This city is my crippled charge.* Konrád's response to the challenge of the city has been to extend its limits to what, before, was hidden or suppressed, thus strengthening the civil society, its language, its possibilities. Literature is its time, its politics, its society, but also, by definition, it goes beyond them to the realm of the unpublished. George Konrád saves himself as a writer and helps his own conflictive world by doing just this.

Carlos Fuentes
University of Cambridge, England, March 1987

THE CITY BUILDER

A flurry at dawn, uncertain hour . . . scarlet light embraces the brick walls. Things swarming out of the shelter of half-light begin their forced orbit. The waste products of comsumption are ready for the garbage truck, the electric pistol for the sedated cattle, eager officers for VHF commands, the unpredictable switchman for steadfast engines. . . . Sleeping eyes are still free from a hail of stimuli, sleeping hands from damp and crumbling matter, sleeping mouths from hostile words and the hurried repertory of curses, pleas, boasts; thighs and testicles from a creeping hand making its uncertain rounds, the organs of the body from warring cells, the brain from a showcase of meaningless parables, terrifying pretenses, anniversary clichés. Per-

spiring skin breathing on crumpled sheets; drooping mouth discoursing with the stale air; nightmares fighting out their battles on the eye's inner field of vision—a limp parcel stamped PERISHABLE. But it is still the uncertain hour, when the shock troops of light invade the furrows of a ravaged face, and each passing second is tapped out on a brain teeming with the slogans of a paltry past.

Snapshots are swimming in fixing solution and are then put in a bulging album that has a certificate of birth on its first page, of death on the last, and a name on the cover: mine. The light of a lantern wanders through a dusty store-room, making endless circles and then focusing on a few privileged objects. Filled with hatred, I take stock of my random memories, scrabbling about carelessly, touching unpleasant surfaces, thinking I ought to turn on the light in the damp, run-down room. Day after day I drag along the dead stock of this giant thriftshop, vowing that one day I will discard all that is useless. I remember things I have never seen; the world is filled with signals, and I let the language of things penetrate me. Solid crusts, walls, and pressure-resistant edifices are shattered by the tremors of my consciousness. And the voiceless barrage does not let up—traffic jams on the road network of the brain, final sale in the window of a burning department store. The clock strikes every fifteen minutes—chapter endings from the dime novel of my dreams. Another morning: I managed once more to traverse the foul-smelling bestiary of my mind.

At exactly 6:00 A.M., high over the mountain, the air-liner breaks through the polar region of fleecy clouds. Bulls of the sky, winged alarm bells, the fourteen-cylinder engines bellow in their pens and upset my dreams. Thirty fragile heads undulate in the air, ride on the current, and find their way into the faint first images of the day. I follow them to the landing strip and stare with impartial concentration at the movement of light on the riveted aluminum flatness, at the elusive patterns of the terrain slipping by underneath. The redundant components of the landscape are stored, perhaps forever, in the deepest recesses of my memory, though from its surface they dry up like raindrops in the sand. The last-minute rush before saying good-bye; you take apart and store a receding face that you never had a chance to observe. Like an unsuspecting smuggler I carry my pictures with me, and consider myself lucky that the customs inspector doesn't make me take out my false teeth.

Requests in four languages are turned on, illuminating strips of frosted glass on the cabin wall. I fasten my seat belts, put out my cigarettes—slight tumbles in the turbulent air, and the uneasy thoughts of arrival are pushed out by the aerial view of a city. Underneath the jagged line of hard-shelled mountaintops and wooded, rocky slopes, we see a glistening tangle of pipes; water tanks look like metallic bomb craters, side-tracked freight cars are filled with tanks. We spot a smoldering pit, smoky-red slag heaps, and silvery-cold storage vans on paved-over grass. Radar screens turn batlike toward us. Soon the city, with its pierced walls, its streets branching out like cracked glass, comes into full view—a wrinkled stone palm, concrete time, apologetic historians' revolving stage. Too much rhetoric, not enough sanity on the silence-craving main square; festive and unhappy ceremonies; opening of cathedrals, power plants, carnivals, parades. And wars, plagues, mass murders, a cavalcade of comic and tragic masks on the reviewing stand, high theatricals, farces, morality plays . . . I step out onto the runway, blinking, feeling the chill. Frayed leaves—lepers on a frozen river—are tossed by the irritable wind; they huddle under the rolling stairway, seeking asylum. The civilian air corridor is empty; before noon only delta-winged bombers, on routine maneuvers, fly in formation over the mountain.

In the sodden garden water drips from the vine, a wasp is dying on the dome of a honey drop; rose scent, like a crazy parachute, hovers over the rosebush, and a grayish-white face recedes into the wall. The crown of mud begins to lift from my brain; through the narrow slits of my half-closed eyes I see the black-hooded, thin-fingered lady emerging from her golden rings. She holds the ascetic baby in her arms and is accompanied by curious birds with singed legs and by root-faced, inconstant saints. Summer is almost over; the glassy shimmer of the afternoon air is trapped between the feet of equestrian statues. Deserted cities and poisoned mother-of-pearl tanks drift over cathedral towers aimed at God. Wild pigeons—these leaflets of immutability, feathery playthings of the early autumn wind—take off from brown roof tiles, their oarlike wings and bewigged lizard heads swaying in the hollow space above the apostles' stone skulls. For brief moments they seem to freeze to the grooves of the church clock, but the clangor erupting from the open belfry shoots them back under the protective helmet of the twin towers. Silver in a field of gray—heraldic animals on morning's airy shield.

Imperial leader in the electric chair, a sentry standing on glowing embers, umbrellas limping in sand, an ermine robe drawn and quartered, a glassy eye seen through a toy gun's sighting slot, carrier pigeons flying through pouring pitch, plastered-over finials, a spaceship gone astray on an unalterable course—all are admitted into the fold. I turn around to look at the ravaged face of a man and remember everything. On his face I can make out the final chapters of Eastern European history, its way of life down to the last coffin nail, its untold mental anguish, its ill-concealed hind thoughts, the well-tended museum of its anxieties, its fits of rage over a strip of grazing land. But he is late; squirming impatiently, he has no time to divest himself of his prison cells. He is still gripped by fear, his face overtaken by a conspiracy of weakness, until finally he, too, comes around to believing that every one of his accusers was right. He has to be careful, as nothing is really his own, not his body or his bed, or even what is said about him; they can do the most dreadful things to him. Should he upset the peace or stand apart, everything he calls his own will leave him, and vengeful knives will flash. Arc lights pick him out, behind each door bloodhounds growl. Layers of protective covering drop away, like his mother's body long ago, and as his own will soon—everything, from teeth to testicles, that ever gave him pleasure. He knows himself, knows what to expect from others who will lay him out on a table, make his fist soft as a feather, surround him with pain, and wrest from him his consciousness.

My mind takes on the city, only to shed it again layer by layer. I might not be able to strip down to a flashlight bulb, for inside the bulb there is only a dark void. A man stands by his bed, fastening and unfastening his buttons. When someone places a hand on him, he looks menacingly at the floor, his whole body waiting to be rid of his well-wisher's touch. But because he has nothing to his name except his hospital pajamas, he just stands there, wondering how many suits of clothes he could take off for good. The prosecutor, for whom I have been waiting so long, may still come; that inquisitor of love, investigator of my freedom, may still show up. He will no longer bury himself in the underground silos of indifference, but will remind me of the burdensome hours of attentiveness, when twelve faces in a streetcar are like twelve devastating questions, when the dark-blue fingers of evening force my eyelids open, when electric news-signs flash death notices on every roof-top, when shadows run me down and masturbating manne-quins in girdles and riding boots get off their rocking horses in shopwindows; when I am afraid I can no longer hold on to anything, and even the plates fall off my table; when I stick out my hand and test the void, because I think I see someone there; when in a minute's time I forget the person who has been whimpering next to me for years, and seize, like a scepter, the unbearable power of existence . . . For a few minutes I feel I can take it: this is what I have lived for; I can check my watch, count my money, ponder over who is fit for what, and realize that in the face of heavy odds I must show the white flag. I am unable to find the right word in the right silence, and mix up even the non-interchangeable faces. All that is left of me is one continuous parody; I exist by virtue of my mistakes. Still, I wait for the prosecutor, who with a single flip of the hand will light up my night. Amid phosphorescent gates and tree trunks, I show him the topography of my pettiness. He occasionally nods at my work, but does not say much. I understand his silence perfectly. With heart-rending cheerfulness the firing squad takes hold of my arm on the freshly sprinkled stone of the prison yard.

I need peace and quiet. As on so many other mornings, I don't feel like wallowing in my abilities. If only the all-devouring locusts of my vanity would disperse, and with a single jerk I could turn myself inside out: if I could free myself from the shivery compulsion of speech, sink my muses in the quicksand of memory, push off from the wet and splintery springboard of nothingness, and for a moment comprehend perhaps the universal laws of drifting and clinging; if, weary of love, I could become a champion of irony and run the shadow plays of history; if for once I could change the imperative mood to declarative; if, knowing that our culture is an obsession, I could myself become an absolute obsession; if, slipping out of my putrid certainties, I could run like a naked pilgrim in one final burst of speed, leaving behind everything that is good, everything that makes *me* good; if I could just run, uncontrolled, afterlifeless, toward the dawn, and when least expecting it, come upon a street, an unnumbered house—I would curl up inside, lock the door, and hold my peace forever.

In ten minutes I will pull myself together. I have, after all, everything I need right here. I slip on my body, my job, my family; I don these rooms, this city; I fill my mouth with clichés. I have no desire to look in the shaving mirror, at a grown man's expectant face which has become my irredeemable charge. Under its eyes I perceive the residue of years past, the runic marks of my unspoken treacheries. After scrubbing it clean, I assume once more this worn but still usable body that at times causes me pain but is all mine. I hold it under the shower, rub it with alcohol and ointments; I stand trapped in the sour smell of old age. Just as an apartment house, or a state, reveals its obsolescence all at once and, after careless use, is plagued by a host of defects—its walls crack, its ornaments crumble, it becomes mustier, draftier by the day—so I become aware of the moral and physical decay of my body. Though it may still be habitable, it is time I slipped out of it. Nothing interests me now as much as this second birth of mine, my release from the clasp of existence. And because we shall soon part ways, I am becoming curious about what we have in common. Today we are still on rather indifferent terms— whether my body is attractive or ugly does not concern me; it takes me where I want to go, doesn't make a spectacle of itself, is not pushed aside, and is approached only by those I want near me. But I do not know any more if it belongs to me or I to it; I depend on it, that much I will admit, but the thought that this shadow in the mirror, this thinning hair, this blinking pair of eyes, these gracelessly dangling genitals, these hardening toenails are the reality of my naked self-awareness seems—though I accept it—rather ridiculous. There will come a time when I will be forced to embrace it, but right now I prefer to have as little to do with this fragile, crushable, flammable entity as with a dull roommate to whom one is bound by the routine of daily living. But if I am not the visible, palpable figure that is imprinted on the minds of other such figures, one that bears the identifying features of my documents; if I will not, even as a matter of convenience, mistake myself for a neighbor who is, after all, the source of many a pleasant sensation, then in whose name do I speak? Bungling exertions, protruding absence, muddled feelers—attempts to discover the self in a few irreducible substances. I am in a dark room that I would gladly leave, but the thought of having no other home holds me back.

Suicide, like painkillers, or the lottery, never interested me. People whose stomachs are pumped want to leave behind their muddled affairs only, and, though angered by the new set of decisions they will have to face, they happily accept the warm bath and the plate of soup. I feel almost free; it seems reassuring that I could disappear at any moment; but though I may be squirming restlessly in my tight shell, a million maddening stimuli a second are still more meaningful than the incomprehensible idea of nothing. I am nevertheless afraid I will dawdle until I miss the right hour, and my place will be taken by an immobilized old man who will have earphones on his pink skull and a bib tied around his neck. His ass will have to be wiped for him, and he will suck on his mushy food with loathsome delight. Perhaps it is only my ignorant pride, but today I am still revolted by the decrepitude of old age, by this obscene and resigned marriage with the traitorous body, by the pathetic uselessness, the diminished intelligence concerned only with survival, the totally uninteresting bulletins about appetite, stool; by the conspicuous haste of examining fingers, the sensuous relief when the wet mattress does not chafe my bedsores; by the pushing out of all my loved ones to the periphery of my vision, since only those have reality for me who stick the rice pudding in my mouth and wash me with lukewarm water. I already hate that bundled-up, parasitic self, and the surrounding slimy aureole of lies, so in this all-important question I would like to come to a decision by myself, and put up with my body only as long as it does its job.

Surrounding my body is an overcrowded apartment into which every day I bring a little more than I weed out. Screened only by my income and inclination, the artifacts of a superannuated culture—concrete proofs of my acts of omission—stream in through the door. They are like promising books I will never master, if only because I don't want to exchange their misery for mine. Undeveloped photographs, faces behind the drawn shutter of emotion: I have seen these faces grow fat and stupid and white on the urine-soaked mattress. (Even in their nightshirts they were difficult to squeeze into their light coffins.) They hover over me in droves and will unmask me sooner or later. There is the telephone, which I usually unplug, lest I keep track of how seldom I receive calls from people to whom I once revealed the transparent depths of my selfishness and stupidity. The creaking bed where I have just about fulfilled my quota of ill-remembered intercourse, and explained in identical words to many a partner that I couldn't live without her, where under a burning lamp the shriek of a new guest meant more than a promotion. (Wandering in their bodies, I sought absolution for my calculated breaches of contract.) Inadequate sedatives for undefined guilt feelings: bottles of liquor drunk to the last, stuporous drop. A table on which I composed my vita in several different versions; a mirror in which I saw myself far too often; old-fashioned Sunday suits that I will not even wear on weekdays; awards for writing junk, for being an accomplice, for simply growing old. Just an apartment where I kept hoarding perishable and useless objects, dust, fear, daily newspapers, man-made noises, incidental flesh; where I surrounded my chilly, porous self with the delusions of a typically vain and stupid era. This is where I was preparing myself to show everyone what I never got around to showing anyone; where I lashed out behind closed doors against heads of state and everyone else I couldn't criticize on the street; where I retreated after my defeats, to toy with my witticisms, my eminently reasonable excuses, with definitions from an otherworldly dictionary; where, while listening to the church clock strike, I realized it was a matter of no consequence what I was good for, or whether I *was* at all. A simple apartment with a multitude of frozen gestures, a bed: massive reminder of deceased love affairs; banished faces that glow in the dark, hurts swept under the rug, a carved horn of plenty filled with disasters, coins hidden under the lilac plant, death throes wrapped in corsets, swaddling clothes, rebellions buried in desk drawers, stubborn marks left by soiled fingers, undiscovered until spring cleaning. An apartment: chronic repository of my forced campaigns, a square-shaped cave whose edges I can make out even in the dark, a furniture fort girding my body, as predictable as my borrowed and thinning thoughts, whose logical flaws and reservoirs of unconscious vibrations make up my partially realized self.

An apartment that has become so familiar I am not aware of it any more, where objects, like pets, grow old with their master and are weighed down by their history—a history undisturbed by revolution, or even a break in the daily routine. Doddering resident of a dilapidated house, I behold the cracks in the wall, as well as those on my mirror image, with moronic mirth. An apartment where provisional weaknesses turned into permanent obsessions, where I once moved in with someone, or took in someone myself, where, considering the time spent within its walls, nothing really happened. It has become like a pair of sensitive artificial limbs, protrusions of my consciousness—I need not look or walk around to come into contact with its objects, its walls. It is the token of my loyalty, burying me deep in this city, as tubers are buried in a hole; inside I can sprout my nightmares. It has taken on my odor, I smell myself in it. Still, I have as little to do with it as with the urn into which they will sweep my remains after cremation.

All around me in this flat is the museum of a dead woman—her souvenirs, her somewhat shabby, rather expensive, and by now probably outmoded clothes, which inspired my workdays and made her, while wearing them, irreproachable. Her mobile face eludes me now; my red-letter dreams simply leaf through the album of her changing expressions. I will not touch her drawers; they guard the materials of a choked memoir, the baroque flourishes of her sloppiness—stockings with runs, tiny teeth in a velvet case, notes on the children's bowel movements. . . . She filled her appointment calendar with reminiscences; clocks offended her pride, and perhaps that is why, like the hands of a clock, she made her rounds in the city every day. With her four wheels she gripped the road, inscribing on it the delirium of speed, the text of her lust. An invalid or a friend: someone was always waiting for her, it moved her to know that she was missed more anxiously than I. An intense presence, enhanced by the staggering mass of her observations, was her one true achievement. Whenever I sat next to her she handed me the name of things about to slip from sight, carefully bathing each word in her mouth. Every evening she came home late: a singing Christmas tree, weighed down by mysterious packages and incredible stories. With a multitude of sound and movement and light she threw the apartment in an uproar; we got dizzy just from watching and listening. I walked behind her like a sluggish Moslem, seeing her grab a bottle of wine, a carnation, a huge piece of meat . . . no man can hold things in his hand that way. She performed her magic slyly, irresistibly; porters, cops, warning signs bowed before her—I knew it, I didn't even have to look. Each moment of her life was a blissful temptation. Fueled by excess heat, she could only sob on all fours, from head to toe, and never was cold in a light jacket. She crashed into a railroad gate, and when in the mood, she made the whole ward laugh. She was indefatigable, and awfully sneaky, when it came to argument, and as vindictive as a thwarted soothsayer. She would nurse her grudges for weeks and then slowly get even for each one. Inexhaustible in her love-making, she was happy if I fell asleep on top of her. I'd feel her incorruptible ass on the street, and she would enjoy being scandalized by my violent intentions. Sometimes I think she still lives here and watches me as I dully go about my business. Then she averts her glance, which, since I don't return it, becomes impassive.

I will survive this light body that lies washed clean on the pathologist's marble table as though waiting for someone. I kiss her mouth, her breast, her foot: a king put his sword between us; she belongs to the marble table. Forty years could do no damage to her, only a single roadside tree, which she, dark schemer, must have picked out long ago. I took away her life, as she did mine; we exchanged cruelty, reluctance, and peace of mind. Maybe if I watch her mouth long enough, she will reveal the name of her warden. I would climb down every shaft, cut across every tunnel; parts of my body would start crawling toward her one by one, on their own. I have already wished to see her dead, buried, forgotten: now she has given me my freedom. In the deepest roots of my dreams, and in the brightest corner of my mind, I could destroy her now. But I exist vertically; I can't stretch out next to her. The baseness of my continuing existence turns my naked face toward the pathologist's mirror on the wall, and I see a mateless animal charred by the red-hot irons of silence. A long hallway in the mirror: a drumbeat, a bit of raw meat, the swish of a whip, the trainer, who always wins, smiles at the empty auditorium. Two doctors enter and take my arms; a hypodermic needle, a trip down the corridor, and I calmly stretch out on the white bed of betrayal.

At 7:45 that morning she crashed into a tree, and at 8:15 her head tossed about lifelessly in the back of a truck. A canvas cloth covered with cement dust was placed under her; the blood trickling from her temple mingled with the cement and became hard. A twenty-year-old stuttering laborer, who had never seen anyone die, could not feel her pulse with his callused fingertips, though she tried to smile at him one last time before her pupils turned back completely. The boy broke off the dark-red pieces of cement and three days later gave them to me in a white handkerchief. When relieved of my chores, my conscious mind becomes a frozen memorial; when I don't quite know who it is that picks up the phone with my hand and talks into it with my mouth; when the train of my daily routine is derailed by signals from some confused automaton and only a dead woman keeps talking and walking in the mirrored hall of my mind; when from the flatness of the ceiling I see myself working, a lonely, quietly scornful man locked in a perspiring body; when in my padded office I reluctantly offer myself a seat behind a table too huge even for my large frame and behave like the absent-minded traveler who misses his train and returns to his hosts, even though they had already said their good-byes; when during a lecture I stop in midsentence because an unexpected bowling ball knocks over all my words; when the sand in the hourglass of my curiosity has trickled down, and there is no one to turn the glass over—at such times I let the bell ring. Standing behind the lit-up window, I just keep shuffling the ashtray on the idle, dusty table.

You return now and then, your entrances are unforgettable; the crack in the door has weight and luster, the air around you sparkles, the doorknob turns for you, the chair rolls under you, even the picture hooks fall off the wall to touch you. Your coat trembles on its hanger and the whole room spins in a whirlpool of good will. Your teeth are still white, your hair black; you eat and drink and stay slim. The smell of skin and perfume is unmistakable, even your belt wears it; one breath tells me you are home. Those marks under your stockings must be my rowdy fingerprints; that little scar at the root of your hair the memory of a wall lamp—you were knocked against it by a blow. What is this peal of laughter about the neighbor's kitten's being chased up a tree by a tomcat? What makes you turn the handle of your teacup always toward my right hand? And why do you have more adventures during a single day than I in a month? What is the meaning of the untraceable flurries of your finger, of those faces, tools, shoes you sculpt out of nothing every second? Why are we sitting in a divorce court, and why did you say inside the courtroom that you can't live with me, and why did I say: Nor I with you? Why do I skirt explanations when every word is a storm trooper, and every sentence a machine-gun nest? Why is it that each breath you take unfolds an interminable tale; why are we so adept at sign language that while we sit in front of the judge and two lawyers, we shoot messages at each other? As you fall asleep under me, your face droops, and in the halo of the night lamp your two strands of gray hair continue your crazy arguments. You wake up screaming, and, with your hands in the air, a glint of fury in your eyes, you try to tell me all at once what you couldn't get across in twenty years. Don't wait for me on the balcony, don't cry into the telephone, don't shoot up my path with clever, reckless, savage telephone calls; don't try to prove that fences are made of gingerbread and you could turn all the traffic lights green just for me. Don't go on deluding yourself that in everything I touch—my ruler, my shaving brush—I can be made to touch you. Disappear for a while, let me forget you, exist as best you can, and as you please, without my constant watch. You slip out of my afternoons and off on your own, you swear, play the whore, store tons of lies in the nimble wrinkles of your nose; but if I grab you by the throat, you can give in fast, and beg and cower, and like a voracious fish make your move, so that in no time you are spread out again on top of me, your two hands clasped around the back of your neck—a black-haired fountain. I succumb to my own self and like a piano and a drum, next to each other, under each other, we keep at it until closing time. You ascend in me like a staircase in a house, binding me even to myself . . . now give me your hand, open your mouth, let me feed you.

Since then I must have shaven four hundred times, eaten as many dinners, and walked around as many times in the empty flat before going to bed. My hair didn't turn gray, my back is not stooped; I wear colorful shirts and ties, have an official passport, crack jokes at conferences, can fall asleep without a sleeping pill. But at times my own voice wakes me: I hear someone howling in my throat, and toward morning I grapple with memories. I can't recall your face, only your latest passport picture; and the more I look at you the denser the fog becomes before my eyes. Each night is taken up by feverish digging; I must force open the floorboards of my mind and dig deep for a corpse. Perhaps age or a stray current will inscribe on my closed eyelids your sweet and dark form; you'll stretch out your legs across my benumbed years, and I'll place you, all of you, between my teeth. I watch the green embers of my cigarette under the red fluorescent light, in a spot marked by your now silent acts of carelessness. In every opened door the snow melts from your hair, and the girl behind you in the café dissolves into slime. I get drunk from a single breath of your presence. Sitting on the floor, I see you lying on your side in bed. There are two hundred faces behind your face, but I am sustained by the lazy, ruffled squeal of one woman. There is nothing of yours I don't like; a 3-D, palpable, smellable movie, you are the prize of my senses, my inalienable example. The paralysis will spread gradually, the doctor said. You smiled a little and didn't wait for it to happen. I see you jumping out of the incinerator; your blue-glazed mask crumbles, and my pulse turns irregular. I take a sniff of your perfume while you watch me from behind your false eyelashes. Then, locking up your remains, I burrow myself into your absence.

An ill-lit room on the drizzly screen. A man is sleeping on a bed, his aging face showing the grooves of tedious events. The frequent rearrangement of his dangling arms, his drawn-up knees, his drooping head, is perhaps synchronized with the swelling of his penis, which forms a tiny grave-mound on the light blanket. A man's bruised fists tie two braids of hair under a woman's chin: a left hook, a bleeding mouth, a startled pair of eyes, a face that's no longer one. The curtain flutters, wind blows through the window. A woman, sitting in an armchair, pensively opens her robe, looks at herself in the mirror before her, at the bluish scar to the left of her navel, at her small, solid, outward-pointing breasts, and musses up her short-cropped reddish pubic hair.

Her legs point skyward behind the windshield of an open car; guttural sounds come from the overturned front seat. It all happened on the road leading from the railroad bed to the game preserve. Behind beehives gone wild and a giant stag raising himself on a signboard. There is a turned-over, wrecked car on the highway, and next to it lies a corpse, her underbelly all exposed. A wasp penetrates her large, fleshy navel. The wrapping paper absorbs the blood. Brake marks, useful to no one but the police, are two wavy lines on the graying asphalt. A seven-armed candelabra circles overhead.

Because it is an extension of my body, my expanding apartment, the scene of my boredom and my anecdotes; because
I know each and every one of its lots, and greet ten thousand faces on its streets, and can smell its stables, barracks,
ghettos, from a thousand miles. Because it was I who gave
its few hundred structures their pleasing or unsightly shape,
because I record its past and plan for its future; because my
blunders, rectifiable only by dynamite, are all lined up in
their concrete armor. Because it is a little shabby, a little
stifling, and makes me wonder why I stayed in it for more
than a week; because there are times when each brick and
cobblestone looks so beautiful I am convinced I can become a part of it, and by relating to its enclosed squares,

TWO

relate to its people. But it is this gossipy provincial town that became part of me, and, while separating me from the world, has also become my world, filling my mind with its jealously guarded fallacies. Its name never appears in the metropolitan dailies, but this is where I learned how historical good will can turn on itself, where I grew stupid and cowardly according to local custom, where my gradual death found its minor coordinates in space. For me this city is a challenge, a parable, an interrogation frozen in space, the messages of my fellow citizens dead and alive, a system of disappearing and regenerating worlds to come, the horizontal delineation of societies replacing one another by sperm, gunfire, senility; a fossilized tug of war, an Eastern European showcase of devastation and reconstruction. One hour out of its existence offends, another consoles, though most often it simply makes me laugh. Because it is the representation of a national character riddled with flaws, which I can recognize in the windows of dress shops and in the caricatures of my dreams. Because by virtue of my practiced clichés I have become one of its shareholders; though beyond the tenuous links of my existence and surroundings, beyond my father's overdecorated gravestone and the haunting shadow of a cremated woman, beyond my hardened and irremediable blueprints, my myopic utopias, and the procession of figures out of an ever-darkening past, I could well ask: what have I to do with this East-Central European city whose every shame I know so well. A city situated between the middle and the end of most scales, its reality far too real—the victim of partitionings, bankruptcies, punitive campaigns, extortions, bombings, burnings; a buffer city, a shelter-belt city, a protective-zone city. It can welcome the enemy with salt and bread, and, having taken crash courses in the art of survival, it can change its greeting signs, statues, scapegoats—its history.

A tent city on the ruins of a Roman circus; ancient cats, crows, lizards scurry over the cracked skulls of legionnaires killed in rear-guard actions. For centuries a sun-faced god on a winged horse led his arrow-shooting nomads and their half-tamed studs from barren plains to vast forests, in search of grass and water, and at last reached this dead city of abandoned Roman watchtowers and water mains, where in the felt tents of their winter quarters they bowed their long, brown heads before the Prince Jesus and built a cathedral for Him from the stones of the old circus. In the undamaged crypts embalmed kings smile with curled-up gums; before their metal caskets tourist-wives stand in awe as flash guns pop and the guide tells them the sad tale of the Tartar invasion. They came from all directions with their battering rams and catapults, their poisoned spears, long, bone-tipped arrows, goatskin tubes, and scaling ladders; their root-eating horses, their cattle trained to screech, their straw dummies strapped to riderless horses and prisoners pulled on chains. They came on windswept, fear-soaked roads aswarm with terrible news. Pouring across the wooden barricades, they slashed the throats of kneeling supplicants. Smoke from scorched villages, burning churches, and the smell of dead bodies floating in the water and blooming in the rye fields trailed in their wake. Up ahead a wall of arrow-absorbing prisoners subsist on sheep guts. A castellan is stretched out between two planks, and on the planks horses pass. Town elders are roasted alive like pigs; citizens are impaled or tied to the wheel, or become lamenting targets in the entryways of their houses. The cathedral, packed with preachers and feuding worshipers, is going up in flames; a rainstorm and human fat put out the glowing embers. But the hordes are already on their way, tracking down the survivors in tree hollows, empty riverbeds, swamps. The murderer cannot rest; whomever he spares will kill him. The city disappears under a sea of weeds, though a few starvelings are already searching under the blackened stones for buried meat and gold coins.

They were succeeded in the main square by the clatter of equestrian statues, the favorites of history books, pulling tumbrels filled with severed heads. Marble-faced generals in their epaulets and decorations receive the homage of subservient anniversaries. Men reduced to street names meet on this square. They hail from the age of nation-state barbarism, from ancient freak-shows, the parade ground of mongoloid oversimplifications, from a school for murder called reality. Destined for great deeds, they make the architects of the city carry lead-heavy rifles and run in knee-high sand, and place dogcatchers in the honor guards, so these men could bark orders during parades. They are the ones who mean murder when they say action, who always inscribe a few solemn, unassailable arguments over the eternal flame of the unknown soldier. Sand-faced leaders, pashas, generals: their entrances mark the dawn of new epochs in my city. I have them to thank for its provincial history—for minor interludes between holocausts, for restitutions going to all corners of the globe. The wheel of history whirs on, grinding up my privileged generation; we trickle into the communicating vessels of movable cemeteries; battles flash by, and anniversaries. Our pillars of smoke are captured on film and kept in archives.

Tonight, the street lights will not be turned on in the main square; passing vehicles will be rerouted, shopwindows and neon signs will remain dark. But the people of the town are crowding behind police lines, the loudspeaker roars pathetic and angry slogans between two marching songs. Fathers lift their sons on their shoulders; expectant mothers shove their way up front, policemen with armbands push back the crowd, which then lets the police cars pass. The chiefs of staff are assembling on the balcony of

City Hall. Balloons, paper hats, and bits of cotton candy whirl overhead. Surrounded by a wall of torches, we await ourselves on the portable reviewing stand. The model society is blaring its horns on the wooden scaffold; approving hands are raised on the flower-bedecked balcony. On cue, the festival begins; let's salute our essential self, wearing borrowed clothes, standing on wooden stilts. Bengal lights frame the tower's dark silhouette; hostile effigies burn atop flagpoles, their obese wax faces melt drop by drop. We stand in a golden aquarium, while fighter planes write flaming letters on a muddy sky and trumpets exult. Now everyone is ready for the oath; on the balcony a solitary voice swears vigilance, and a square-shaped column of torches echoes it. In an age of satellite-relayed exchanges of ideas, the torch bearers vow allegiance to the barbed wire. Let's tell stories, celebrate with drinks, accept handouts and decorations. Let's not be frightened of the cannon salute, and at the banquet table, let's dig in.

The unknown subject's life-size statue stands at ease in the main square, where superior force has found it pleasant enough to enter; official seals, interpreters, spokesmen were always readily available. Attaché case, letter of recommendation, decayed wisdom tooth, scatological jokes, mild reservations, key to a fully furnished apartment, at whose door revolution and war in full armor never knock. My fellow citizen has no reason to be dissatisfied: he has no chronic ailments, only a growing bank account. He'll do his own vacuuming when he retires. On bedclothes-smelling evenings, when police cars cruise with slackened vigilance in the knocked-up city, he operates his sexual apparatus calmly. When he eats or listens to religious music, his face relaxes; he looks at the bright side of things and votes for the official candidate. When asked by higher officials, he tells all he knows about almost everyone, and completes the castigating sentences of his superiors with eager self-criticism. Now if they would just double his salary, he would be happy. He let his brother know, when he asked to be visited in prison at Easter, that he'd rather spend the carfare on shoes for the prisoner's child. He will not take in his fugitive friend for the night—let him face the music. At the incriminating hearing he said of his onetime boss that he had reeked of treachery from the start; now he has the proof—they hanged the man. He has a healthy regard for the day's, the week's reality, but does not have the guts to think with long-term sobriety. He has to belong somewhere, and it's foolish to resist the powerful. True, they are quick to anger, but if he can't mollify them, he lies on the rack and reviles himself. Whoever is too proud gets his nose rubbed in the muck; might makes right; a family man laughs up his sleeve when the scatterbrained is about to pay with his life. When the town changes hands he sees what is worth snatching in no man's land, in the lower depths of empires. Good and bad depend on who stands guard in front of City Hall; anything your friend knows, every idiot will find out; a manacled neighbor is not worth a greeting; if he swings on the gallows, it's no sin to steal his pants—he won't mind the wind blowing across his thighs. After a crushed rebellion, when everyone who was mixed up in it is busily plotting against everyone else, he clings to the paving blocks of the town square, convinced that embraces, not struggles, help one survive the conquerors. Recurring humiliations—he endured a great many—are the cornerstones of his trust, and they fade away in the stillness of time like noonday bells.

Nine hundred feet above sea level, above knife-sharp towers and cranes that look like rows of gallows, above green lambs huddling on the mountainside, on top of a large exhibition hall, above the optical dialogue of interconnecting logs and blocks, from the vantage point of seagulls and cormorants, and the heights of aerial maps and self-surrender, from where the city is one clamorous sentence in which a merry-go-round and a hearse constitute a single predicate, I take anniversary pictures of my provincial town with the telephoto lens of my mind. Because I am a city planner it proves to be an immensely difficult task. I bore the giant lens into its flesh; unable either to rearrange or to abandon it, I keep photographing it—surreptitiously, spitefully. I grow weak in the sunlit timelessness—a sign of old age, I guess. Death comes but once, but here the seasons touch one another . . . a gardener's wisdom, I'll reject it in a half hour. A planner can neither improve things nor make them much worse.

Blown-up images of the city give rise to stupid thoughts, and vapid visions—to the inane plans of engineers, masons, patresfamilias. A few years ago I flew over it in a helicopter with fellow city planners. Why couldn't all this be different, we asked; why should this house, this street, stay where it is? An unjustifiable, irrational city—untidy, crowded, anarchic. Let's put air ducts into its gasping lungs; let's relieve its clogged arteries and cut through its concentric circles. Traffic is choking its inner core; it is cowardly and sentimental to want to spare its undulating and redundant mysteries. This is the eleventh hour, time for major surgery. We managed to rearrange the city down to the last grain of sand. Upheavals of imagination erupted under our fingers. Then we came down and saw under our giant dragonfly mountains of smoke, whirling dust.

In a few months the room-sized replica of the town, made of clay, wood, and foam rubber, was completed. The woefully accurate scale model of two crazy little sculptors, it was first daubed with oil paint, then sanded down to make it look a little worn. We swung over it in rubber chairs, like infants learning how to walk, and had fun trying out the acrobatics of weightlessness. We lifted out parts we didn't fancy, then carefully put them back. As we fluttered and balanced above irrefutable injuries to the builder's ethic, above the flotsam of thoughtless plans, we began to approach what we had a little more carefully. The dictator of perfect arches and angles vanished from our minds; we were careful now in putting our hand on the unaccustomed body of time, and no longer wanted to imprint our thought patterns on its dense configurations. For though the city was at the mercy of our remodeling furor, and we could have imposed our simplistic solutions on the terrain, we were getting more and more anxious, and idly flapped about over this disconcerting model. Let's face it: we liked this city; it resembled us, and the colored drawings of children on gray asphalt. We began to look into the labyrinthine streets and saw witty and mostly unorthodox solutions to tricky tasks, to which patient time had given its stamp of approval. We saw limber channels of motion amid stiff blocks. . . . We even accepted the scattered bones in excavation ditches, accepted this complicated piece of work that has accommodated so much havoc, so much change, and that has come to resemble only itself. It has weathered, and profited from, the many gifts it has received—comely ones from men of talent, abominations from the unscrupulous. It also survived the marks of our bungled efforts, the decaying signs of would-be uniqueness, conflagrations, explosions. We watched a graceless community's obstinate dialogue with its surroundings—a palpable, though crumbling, piece of history, able to survive all—an obsession we could always reconstruct from rubble. Finally, we did manage to alter it. In making our contribution we were neither proud nor meticulous, and took the risk of our grandchildren's ridicule or pity. It's not they we are working for; a city built for the future is unlivable, a reality only for eccentric planners. So we thought up bogus schemes, did what we could for our fellow citizens, as best we could, without shame.

The city is a coupling of stone and light under my balcony, a stretched-out body in the folds of a mountain, poeticized matter, a trading post for signals, the rotating drum of risks, a clanging, rumbling pool table, a moment's freedom in a forced march, a chess game played by learning machines against unbeatable time, counternature formed by formulas and refuse, rollerskating houses, wavy sidewalks, streetcars rattling on sundry tracks, three hundred thousand distorting mirrors quick to take offense, three hundred thousand pompous jokes wrapped in ready-made suits and TV tubes, a Ferris wheel stuck in midair, a rifle range where the marksmen stand in a circle and aim their guns at one another, a spooky train-ride through workshops, council chambers, bedrooms, a wardrobe filled with outlandish costumes, where each face hypocritically takes off its masks, where pillar saints, bemedaled generals, and honorary presidents on beflagged rostrums are crossed off by a white paintbrush, a dusty, bespittled, and somewhat stifling all-night movie theater where they end up showing movies brought in by the viewers, a hundred thousand private sports arenas for ongoing showdowns between the sexes and differing age groups, a subterranean struggle against four horsemen, charging across the skies with comets, solar storms, space stations, plague-carrying clouds, contaminated rain, industrial waste. Sometimes I think I live because of it; at other times I am convinced I live in spite of it, but with it surely, like an invalid with his wheelchair.

Its inhabitants live their European middle-class lives, managing their affairs in the hope of daily resurrection. They have been transferred into their objects, and exist through them, for them. They exist, therefore they are needed, and though they may not know by whom, until their uncertainty is resolved, they go on accumulating painless stimuli and special distinguishing marks. They appear wherever they are expected, traveling from inadequate apartments to inadequate jobs, the decision makers in automobiles, the redundant masses in streetcars. Depending on their station, they press keys or levers, serving a giant enterprise that has outgrown itself but that, with its flabby idiosyncrasies, controls their vitals. With decreasing efficiency, and according to increasingly cumbersome regulations, they turn out objects and concepts; out of sheer habit they fashion morose and malleable contraptions. They are lent out by the employer to themselves from afternoon to morning; it is hoped they won't forget their mentors. Whoever remembers best gets to own a car; the one who doesn't, can't even afford a movie, and has a punctilious sergeant checking up on him at night to see if he is really in bed at ten, watching TV. His share of the national income roughly describes his furniture, his books, his supper, his desires. This is a $750 town, inhabited by $750 people who would like to be worth $1,000. Their shops, theaters, beds are filled with the psalms of mediocrity. Caught in their repetitive duties and a constant time squeeze, in their perishable, nervous bodies and in the web of their apartments and cities, they acquire, minute by minute, the knowledge of their death. Stockpiling their unsolved problems, they deceive one another and fume endlessly. Searching for the name of their nameless losses, they dream of enemies—if they could eliminate just that one, their existence here would be justified. They can satisfy their nagging envy only by forcing one another to observe new prohibitions; their thirst for revenge outweighs police efforts, informers outnumber victims. They like to bow before their assertive double, whom their quarrelsome imagination endows with traits lacking in their own provisional selves. They put his statue, his photograph or painted likeness above their bed or on their table, and in their weakness ask him for strength. If members of their family are bored with them, they would like at least to identify with their exaggerated mirror image and hear him say that the fellow feeling is mutual, and that they are indispensable just as they are. Members of a helpless community, they are too timid to love one another and are always waiting for the prodding of uniformed men. I would gladly push this city aside—its objects, its people, its heaps of documents and stones, and would watch, like an outsider in front of a courthouse, its slow eviction, and the mercenary wind as it blows the dust of an unuttered verdict onto its crumbling walls.

I could go anywhere; in my suitcase and in the furrows of my brow I carry my city with me. Like a character flaw it has become a part of me, and though I may disguise it, I can no longer tell us apart. The main highways pass it by, visitors can cover it in a few hours, and realize after a day that everything they find out about it is a repetition. Only its inhabitants are interested in this town, not even they, really. A small-town ball game, during the second half of which the losing home team lolls about the muddy field. A neglected, morose, nervous city that dreads decisions, loathes to call things by their name, forgets its vows, and rubs elbows with its betters, whom it imitates and hates. It never got over the fact that in the card game of history it was always dealt a bad hand. It wastes its people and pays double time for everything. Half the day is spent here by going through the motions of life, miming work, marking time. I am fed up with its oversensitive self-deceptions, its cunning defense of submissiveness, its admiration for delusions believed to be reality; with its carefully worked-out cycle of arrogant truancy, sneaky revenge, spiteful adages with which it admonishes its teachers: Today is my turn, tomorrow will be yours. My hands stretch far, I'll strike back. I will gladly have nothing as long as you have nothing. We drink from the same cup, crap in the same pit; if you insist on sticking out, take what's coming to you. As I grow old and senile, I can barely see beyond my kinfolk. On the day of reckoning I will be surrounded by the snipers of bureaucratic jungle warfare, and breast-beaters lowering their pants at the sight of a raised cane; and by the winking henchmen and blood-pact-signing false witnesses who at the very first interrogation incriminate me indiscriminately; the showmen of integrity, the moralizing yes-men, the daring shelter-seekers, well-informed and opinionated janitors, the champions of abandoned property for whom each turmoil is a good occasion for plunder. The mousehole philosophers who, to escape censure, offer their services to the cat, and the pillar saints of frankness who gather the people of the marketplace around them to let them know in sign language how much they have had to suffer for their outspokenness. It's absurd, but these are my prized possessions; I don't want to forget any of them. A stale thesis-play is being performed in the open-air theater of my face, the most disgusting buffoon makes me laugh; but as soon as the hypocrites leave, the stage is enveloped in darkness.

Early in the morning, when still in bed, I would like to travel—if only there were someone to tell me where to go. The conductor is about to blow his whistle on the departure platform of the railroad station. The remote-control switch clears the way for the blue-and-yellow cars of the morning trains. I wipe the froth off my mouth in front of the shiny coffee-dispenser and take possession of my privileged or disadvantaged but in any case numbered seat. I spread out the mock events of play history on my lap, turn on the pseudo news in my pocket. With a few constrained sentences I seal under glass the fixed smiles of my travel companions, and lean back among the phantoms of my oaths and revenges. I overhear a schoolmaster's endless admonitions to a children's choir, and pause to look at the machine-gun-carrying border guards as they tend their bloodhoundlike majors. Just before the final whistle, heeding the insinuation of an empty booth, I ask forgiveness, or swear devotion, one last time to an offended telephone receiver; then I block out the house I have just left, along with its inhabitants and passions. Pushing back my memories, I take my seat in a present tense that stretches to the end of the horizon, and ready myself for an amusement park of challenges, spectacles, confrontations. I shut the door on the express train of time moments before departure, and, looking over electric carts crisscrossing the station with uncharged batteries, I lean out into the rusty steam.

After the war, shepherds used to rest their lust-filled heads on molehills along the tracks, but now, in place of meadows floating under a hawk's stare, and beaver lodges nestled under cane stumps, factories sprinkled with tile and glass bricks are melting in the sunshine. Four coils of steampipes run across their facade, and giant cranes insert standardized panels between concrete blocks that stride toward the sky. A sluggish yellow wind licks the sulphurous vapors. Industrial cathedrals on expropriated wheatlands, the sacred cows of an industrial age come to a close—unbreakable, self-feeding piggy-banks, barely profitable memorials to the unknown soldiers of a generation. Unimaginatively, gropingly, they manage to produce things here, though the end product is often worth less than its component parts. Still, they divide the landscape; above them rise the sleek, new office buildings, and the tubercular antiaircraft guns of the skyward-pointing smokestacks. My mind's eye sees outmoded machinery being replaced by outmoded machinery, the metamorphosis of private dwellings into public office space. An apartment built to last a hundred years is today's luxury, a machine that becomes obsolete in less than ten years is tomorrow's nest egg. They have moderate resistance to heat, wear, and acids; their sensors signal gross errors. Abused themselves, they now and then maim their overworked operators. These were the idols of my generation, these unwieldy, inefficient machines. They amuse my straying glance, but my sympathy dries up as soon as I take a closer look at the power-play-concealing pseudo designs, at the uniform roughness of supporting and cable-camouflaging columns, at auxiliary systems buried in concrete for the sake of a fancy façade, at the ostentatiously elevated roofing, at the official time-and-resource-squandering prestige architecture that enjoys the favors of a deficit economy. To my engineer's mind this kind of grandiloquent construction is a moral flaw. I see a new order emerging from authority-sanctioned irresponsibility, from the I-tell-you-nothing-you-tell-me-nothing cynicism of those who are chosen for their idle chatter, and who lie low behind the protective shield of organizations and speeches—a new order from the good-natured pardoning of every large-scale wastefulness, the price for which is paid by the sullen shadows glued to those machines. My extended technical logic tells me that the rule of the skeptical majority means getting the best results with the smallest expenditure. Prodigality is exploitation even if no one benefits from it.

But since these would-be factories are no more useless than a baroque stable made of marble, and because in the message conveyed by objects even redundancies are significant, and because whatever I consider useful is only that until I test it, these rattling industrial statues impart meaning to a pile of discarded bricks on the burned-out grass, to the iron pillars torn from the ground along with their concrete pedestals, to oxygen cylinders buried in sand, and to abandoned cranes and road-paving equipment, kept idle by a shortage of parts. In junk yards, scrap-chewing machines are digesting the disabled soldiers of yesterday's technology; doorless one-family houses, with the picture of a soldier on the inside, last year's draft notices on the outside wall, fall flat in front of bulldozers. On a half-cleared pile, the carriage of the former landlord is raising its shaft toward us; the horses were unharnessed by extensive industrialization. This is where my grandfather's estate, with its cricket course and garden pavilion, used to be, where the longest-named ladies of the town applauded a fashion designer's latest creations: knee-length bathing suits and incredibly artistic hairpieces. I gladly exchange their flowery presence for the boom of the excavator. Let the dumpers dump their rocky, stinking, contaminated soil. Let an entire industrial infrastructure with its far-flung networks spring forth from the bucolic land; and on railroad lines illuminated by mercury-vapor lamps let crack trains roar by with double rows of even faster automobiles on their backs. Between broken-down railroad cars and water ditches trembling in slag, we keep increasing the ratio between time and distance, and pass from violated space to the imaginary terrain of a mind inhabited by antediluvian animals. And although the steam whistle near the chimney top has gone to seed, all this is more appropriate here than a plow drawn by oxen. With fire from the blast furnace, a flaming torch and wires crackling with masculine ideas, the sun king overthrew the rule of the moon-earth-water princess. Something had to happen and more or less did.

I walk past my father's first creation: the pyramidal old power plant. For six decades this piston kept the city alive: linear motions in the steam cylinder were turned to circular ones by giant connecting rods. I am baffled by the neo-Romanesque, bastionlike tower above the plant, by the saw-toothed cornices, the arched rows of windows. What did my father want to express with all this? As the son of the architect I could sit in a little booth high above the mine train, in front of the coal wagons that ran on rails and screeched happily between the loading station and the coal mounds. I loved the taut cables on the cone-shaped, mitered chimney, the cellular stained windows on the palatial turbine house. The oversized brick facing was designed for monstrous machines; with plenty of raw material at our disposal, a modest degree of efficiency was good enough. I am moved by my father's vacillation; he felt one had to build shelters not for animals, people, gods, but for machines. Still, this shelter became my feudal castle, my playground. Next year we shall tear it down: it consumes too much coal and produces little electricity. If the machinery looks ridiculous, so does the engineer. Cybernetic planning is no more than a dream for me: my students did a better job designing the arched roof of the new power plant than I ever could. In the battle against obsolescence only the knowledge of its reality remains unscathed.

In the workers' cottages along the railroad tracks, the intolerable clatter of pneumatic drills, the sizzle of sparks, the whining siren atop the watchtower finally abate. This is their home, the home of those who, while rolling iron-clasped crates with foreign inscriptions, look up at the giant airliners and know they will forever be looking at them from below. Before the formal opening of the new plant, at which I accept a silver cup in behalf of technical progress, I look around in the old shop where I worked for a few months after being released from jail. They accepted me because they knew where I had come from, and avoided me because they knew that mine was but a brief stay amid the unchanging scenery of their lives. I find my old milling machine; it has been working reliably for forty years, only now my successor has to operate two of these monsters at double speed while standing in a hail of sparks. He could be my son. He has been building a cottage for four years. He takes tranquilizers. He is balding. The disorder is the same, only the objects creating it changed. Grimy twists of cable in a corner, scattered pieces of chain, steel shavings in a tin drum, oily paper rags, a vermilion-colored ladder, rusty wires, battered coalbins, and a new addition: a bicycle rack fastened to the concrete floor of the locker room and a stone flower-stand with a trace of something green inside. Stalin disappeared from the bulletin board, only the exiled young Lenin is still there, a hunter's gun on his shoulder and his arms around his wife. Looking at the turbulent Yenisei, he smiles knowingly, though there is a lot he doesn't know. We completed the three-chambered machine shop. Our staff is small, the degree of mechanization high. Noxious fumes and smells are sucked out, noises muffled. There are skylights and climate controls. We eliminated the inefficient handling of material with an overhead trolley in the middle chamber. The wall is covered with yellow tile; the machines are navy-blue, the work clothes apple-green, although the people wearing them will not earn more than they did before. The supervisors subdivide tasks taking less than a minute to complete; the more sophisticated the tools the workers use, the less meaningful their work becomes. A toddler could be trained in two weeks to perform these tasks. The workers' knowledge of materials and processes is fast waning; with a single motion they pass tiny units on through an ear-splitting tunnel of sound to join unknown end-products. The persistently dull worker likes this; he asks no questions, makes no waves; his brain is like a broken record, repeating the same phrase over and over. He only responds to basic stimuli and believes this is the natural order of things. He exists when he doesn't work, or when he fantasizes about genitals. Arthritis, slipped disc, contracture, I'll-show-them fits, I'm-nothing apathy, jealous nightmares—people locked in their bodies, representative types from the industrial Middle Ages whose brains were expropriated by the state. As they get older, their paychecks get smaller—they are shadows of a central pseudo-consciousness. In their hands only the actual pieces of work change, never the instruments of production. They themselves could be simplified until they won't feel like defending themselves, or sit in front of the glittering instrument panels of machines powered by the light of the moon, or control single occurrences within complex systems, with the aid of computers capable of directing automated production schemes and storing on their magnetic tapes entire processes of physical and chemical creation. *Their* skills are inscribed on their foreheads. I can work even while taking a walk; they, only when the machine is turned on. My work is more complicated than I am; theirs is simpler than they are. Yet I am not about to prove to them that it is still they who have the upper hand; I can live without such proof myself. Misleading them, I also mislead myself. Beyond our common concern for public property, we choose our separate interests. By depending on me, they might get a raw deal; let them learn to fend for themselves. If they say yes to everything, I will grow flabby, and the stupidest go-getters of my class will get the better of me. An over-worked, blankly staring face turns toward me; I could see it spent a long time among heavy, oily, hurtful objects. The money that worker makes is more than well earned, but he has no room to let go in, no chance to be extravagant. His tomorrow is not a continuation of today but its replacement.

I wander in and out of flooded villages in a motorboat, floating on hopeless waters. Shivering foxes and fallow deer swim toward oak trees immersed up to the crown. Scores of horses follow a stallion in wedge formation above disappearing wells, sties, hothouses. A wolf cub shakes its fur on a drifting roof, ducks navigate among Bibles, sows, still in their pen, sway in the water, their teats turned toward the sky. At the foot of the church the roar of a waterfall is heard. Cattle are chewing mud and in their hunger bite one another. A rail car, sunk axle-deep in the now tranquil water, speeds along shrunken telegraph poles. The rescue operation is just about over. As leader of a defense team, chosen for lack of anyone better, I look around to see what can be saved. My ferryboat passes through deserted villages; as the waves hit the lit-up houses, these collapse with a shudder. Between beams coming asunder, a pillow, a hat flutter down a watery street. A school is immersed to the eaves, its ceiling held up by a large map-cabinet. A tiny pennant has stuck to the eye of a drowning ox. Between two poplar trees a trailer-truck is parked; the two drivers sit and smoke on the top of the driver's cabin, their bread and canned meat right beside them. They look at the clattering helicopter under the rain clouds, and at the crumbling homes being tossed all around. Appreciating the humor of devastation, they keep eating, and chase away the rescue soldiers from their side. Next to tall, dense pine trees a dead gypsy sways in a washtub. Water stagnates; birds throng in black spirals above contaminated eels.

I am riding on the circular dam of a village whose women would not be evacuated. A thousand people in all, they'd eat anything. A kettle filled with mutton stew has stood in the schoolyard for a whole week. A heavy downpour soaks the spongy embankments, extinguishing torches set in the mud. A pile driver arrives; we work through the night under floodlights. The rushing water washes away soaked clumps of clay. Next to the defensive village a flock of sheep, each with its head buried in another's belly, is floating downstream on a raft, followed by a carved church-steeple. I am drunk from plum brandy and fatigue; my motorcycle moves by itself on a dike that rises only a few inches above water. Expectant eyes wake me: their gentleness is oppressive. On bars slung over their shoulders they carry pails full of garden soil for the dam. No army was ever so disciplined; they would let me have their own beds, and wouldn't dream of leaving their posts. Thanks to them, the jittery cow can stay in its dry shed. An old man rolls a cigarette and passes it around. I have an apple and pass that around. Someone produces a bottle; the back of a human being feels warm now, his breath doesn't disgust me. When the floodwaters recede, flattened mud walls will be replaced by a brick house. We will clean out the wells, build a taller embankment, plant a new apple tree, drink May wine on the cement porch, and gaze in amazement at a wolf. On the doilies of the new china-closet, porcelain fiddlers in wigs and tailcoats will play a song about the longings of a lazy summer. Those who are so tender now will learn to hate me when they find out that I shortened the sidewalk in front of their property. I must build the brick foundations for their new houses on stilts. Taking an impartial look at the village from the window of my car, I may even recognize them and greet them with a quick smile.

As the water settles, uniform mud-piles line the streets of a village soaked to nothing. I stand on the muddy highway as suntanned, fleshy faces commiserate from inside slowly moving automobiles with official license plates. The local people are not allowed to return; there are DANGER signs all over. Still, in small groups between the tracks, and bared up to their thighs, they sneak back, and above the washed-out railroad bed they walk gingerly on the crossties, avoiding the irritable guards on the roads and intersections. They steal into the contaminated area, back to carrion and garbage. From a life's work that dropped back to its original formlessness, they try to salvage what's salvageable. Over on the roadside there is a scrubbed kitchen-table, a sewing machine, a fishing boat; on them a slimy piece of smoked bacon, a few ears of corn with mud lodged between the grains, soft, blistery family-portraits, a rosary on a chipped plate, and a leather-bound keepsake album from whose dog-eared pages the secrets of peacetime were washed away, made forever illegible, by the water. Squatting on a cupboard in their garden lake, women are rinsing a gray ball of rags; a dog is swimming after a picture frame; a child's shirt is hung up to dry on naked apple trees; a man puts back the telegraph pole, then tries to dry a radio—maybe it'll work one day. From the mud he pulls out a piece of tile, from the mouth of a corpse a gold tooth. Jokes are made about lost trousseaux, champagne glasses; humor travels from door to door, it's as if a campful of kids were having fun on the open road. Neighbors stand behind women whose asses point skyward, and pinch their soft, clayey thighs. A closed blue car, as big as a bus, arrives. Men in white rubber suits search in waist-high water for decomposing carrion. With a hook and rope they drag a bloated cow into their car; a few minutes later its owner receives a bagful of ashes. A pickax turns up an old man; he lies face down in the mud, clutching under his shirt a cup he won in a cross-country race of old. The cup cannot be pulled out of his hand. The man in the rubber suit says he is sorry: he is not allowed to cremate humans. The water is contaminated, there is no stove, ducks are cooked in wine reserved for mass. In the tall brick rectory the parish priest, freed from the evangelical custody of old women, offers his church to faithful and faithless alike. He senses there is no connection between providence and the flood. God didn't create this world; the world created God; goodness is indivisible. He smiles timidly; if not for the great turmoil, the community would never have witnessed this confession of heterodoxy, and would have been the poorer for it.

These people don't need my pity; they feel at home in their calamity. I return to my car, which boasts an official license plate. I will redesign this village, though it will not be easy to please them. Beyond the railroad gates, guards with machine guns are escorting a group of gypsies. Last year their shacks were set on fire, and they were ordered to move on. Now they weep over the pits they hollowed out

of sand. The guard says they are suspected of having ty-
phoid fever, but the group is frantic. Fearing execution,
they implore me to set them free. I tell them they are only
being taken to a disinfecting station where they'll get
blankets and clothes. They look at one another, and at me;
then a woman falls on her knees: At least spare my child. I
leave them. With rolling eyes they keep tearing their ker-
chiefs and shout after me: Lick my shit. I am tired;
through the car window I can see the crown of an oak
tree—it erects itself, multiplies its branches in the light. A
rebuttal amid the ruins. What the priest calls God is the
faint possibility of a world inherent in temporary configurations.

With his long hammer, the axle-tapper in his raincoat
bends down under my window. The grating of metal in the
drizzly fog; sooty warehouses with green iron doors; waiting
cold-storage vans loaded with frozen meat, assault guns
covered with canvas, a sugar-beet hill at the foot of a sloping chute. A military camp in a mountain clearing; white-
washed brick facing beneath the watchtowers. The woods
are off limits to strangers. In natural caves, an underground
factory—one of my earliest designs; there was good money
in it. Protected, specially marked deer in front of the privileged hunters' jeep; the shiny globe of water tanks behind
newly designed villages; a sprinkler's jet going around and
around between poplars combed southward by a gentle
wind. Dwarf peach trees stretching across rocky plains; behind them a peasant-baroque church steeple. Familiar-look-
ing women standing amid girlish strips of seedling forests
and in hothouses covered with inflatable synthetic tunnels.
Streets without gutters, backyard sewage purifiers, a vine
arbor made of stolen pipes; carnation and asparagus growing in makeshift hothouses. A man who built an entire wall
from plunder and trained his tea roses on porcelain insu-
lators swiped from the factory is dozing in the shade, a

newspaper covering his face. Others are painting, planting, polishing—every stick of wood is worth something. A piece of tile, a flower stand, new shades on a tiny house—so many private wrinkles in the immense uniformity. The ground plan for an inquisitive life emerges from under wrinkled brown hands, in room-sized plots. Fresh tummies exhibit their roundness in kitchen doors, a tin tub sits on the gravel path; in it a child grabs at a sparrow. A ping-pong paddle keeps tapping on well-nourished thighs, between daisies and the sound of a tape recorder. Framed by curls like bunches of grapes, a nursing mother drinks her coffee and enjoys the sun before doing the wash. Serene in his knowledge of his fate, the father watches her effusive hips as she bends over the baby carriage. He would be suspicious of her if she were to put up with his whims in bed, but what the flagging instinct prescribes, he obligingly, if hurriedly, attends to. He can never hope to have more than what he has, and has no choice but to stay with his wife and two children, for with his income cut in half and no place of his own, he could only find an angrier, staler woman. Self-taught men of consumption, they have to eat to lessen tension. Beyond poverty's self-control, they establish, in yesteryear's seedy attire, the absolute rule of petty gluttonies. The women here have gold teeth, but in half the homes there are no books. A hundred lives pass amid tawdry knickknacks before a new thought appears. After work, thirty-year-old men lean on fences along unpaved roads, and know exactly what is in store for them, down to their third-class funeral. For only one out of every twenty young men or women is there a college education, a new apartment, new horizons; chances for a new start are remote enough to hurt. (Wall inscriptions here proclaim only the names of soccer players.) Whoever finds his shame burdensome makes a separate peace with his reality and uneasily takes his place midway between what is desirable and what is deadly. Every twentieth man or woman is aware of his chances and sooner or later moves away. In their new, freer homes they dream of a slightly less predictable future.

Scattered, grayish-brown islands in the subsiding river. In the marsh a motionless male back on a fish-feeding raft, and a somber cluster of cattails. Unreal-looking orange-red trailer-trucks on the silvery highways. I finally decided to move the village onto a hill, far above the flood land. Unplastered houses; well caissons. On the edge of the plowed stubble a fox is chasing a pheasant cock; yesterday's plowland turned gray; today's is blacker. The sausagelike clumps of soil have cracked. An old man leads a child by the hand on the highway; they watch the train and wave, though no one waves back. Scrawny geese hover over a stick brandished by an old woman. Cylinder-shaped concrete cloaks of grain silos; huge piles of apples looking like gabled roofs. Women in rubber boots are shoveling them, perhaps onto the conveyor belt of a distillery. Telephone lines on concrete poles, tottering calvaries at the foot of a red-capped tower, a grazing white colt between two soccer goalposts. An area becoming industrial in fits and starts: challenging mechanisms, the finger marks of concern, collapsing evidences of carelessness. Interchangeable work and holidays, the banquets of East European corruption, sated crows on a cracked highway dimly lit by the flickering hurricane lamp of a farm wagon. Calamity's panoramas were removed tracelessly by the scenery-shifting stage crew.

The train comes to a halt at the frontier station. Armed guards line up on both sides, from the locomotive all the way to the last car, and send back passengers stepping off the train to get drinking water. Behind me a young man in a flat service-cap shines a flashlight under each seat, then another appears and does the same. Sound of a whistle and words of command are heard from outside; my fellow passengers rub their palms against the legs of their pants. Someone is taken off the train; he is asked to remove his glasses and is identified as the figure on a blurry photograph. The formalities of the inspection are over, the train lurches forward. We pass between wooden watchtowers, electronic wires strung between concrete poles, and child-faced soldiers riding on horses near the tracks. In their terrain-colored raincoats they disappear behind an abandoned shed in the deep-red thicket, their machine guns slung across their chests. Both I and my fellow travelers have the same thought at this moment.

On my arrival, before catching a cab, I put down my briefcase and stand in line for a glass of beer in the waiting room. By the time I finish drinking I have had a tiff with an irritable tourist and taken a random survey of the crowd. What I see is neither beautiful nor ugly, simply a mode of production, a structure of power. We mean something to one another, but in order to extricate myself from the structure I must realize I am stuck in it like a nail in a board. Flash guns pop, lighting up the faces. The waiting room is divided into three areas: to the right is the bar, in the middle the passageway to the tracks, on the left, benches, all of them taken. Some people lean against the wall and sleep standing up, like horses. Four loaders, their hair white with flour, join hands and sing. Holding a beer bottle in one hand, they turn to one another and exchange sorrowful kisses. A drunken man wants to shake hands with everyone; he offers his pocket watch for sale and is waved away: he smells of urine. But he defends himself solemnly: he is a Hungarian in body and soul, his hands, too, and he holds them out, defiant in his grief. There is only one old man who pays any attention to the drunk. He stands here by the iron stove all year round, showing off the silk lining of the coat he got from his officer son. Now he takes out a transistor radio, puts it to his ear, and shakes it, but no sound comes out so he tucks it away. He got the radio, too, from his son. Smoke from a stack covers with soot the walls of nearby houses and the windows of the waiting room. At the bus stop people look above one another's heads; a young man drops his match on his neighbor's foot, a mine goes off—sweaty faces, eyes that see no one, an assortment of suppressed hurts turn on one another. On the greasy pavement things start happening; under every shirt crouches a death sentence. A country gypsy tells his friend that he found lodging in an attic. The other would like to know if he could move there, too, for he lives with five others in a circus wagon, on which his factory's labor-relations office hung a sign: WORKERS' HOSTEL #3. The attic dweller is reluctant to invite him, whereupon the wagon dweller starts boasting. Not far from his home there is a signpost with a picture of a camera and a line drawn across it. Behind the sign a scrap yard and an elevator that takes you down to an underground factory. The other simply says that where he lives there is a deep pit with many large holes in its wall. Once when he was walking there he saw a girl lying in a deck chair at the bottom of the pit. She asked him: What time is it, young man? And then: You want to hear the truth? Should I tell your fortune? Since then she climbs up to him on the attic ladder every night. Nobody can make you pick up a bleeding body, says a truck driver. His friend is skeptical. What if his life depended on it? Let the ambulance take care of him. What if it doesn't come? asks the friend. The truck driver pulls his peaked cap over his rheumy eyes. Nobody would pick me up, either, believe you me. The other is insistent. I would. I don't even like to fuck any more, says an electrician; fishing is better. But women won't let you have a moment's peace. His friend is not convinced. We can't keep still, either. See that woman in the ticket booth? On the train we'll lock ourselves in the john. The electrician doesn't care for the setting. It's a very good spot, insists his friend, you can even wash up. My wife doesn't let me sleep, the electrician says sadly. Sleeping is better, too. She'll be pestering me even in the grave; they'll put her coffin right on top of me. An old man chatters into his beard, binds his wire-rimmed glasses to his ear with a string, and breaks off a piece of cheese and bread with his yellow fingers. He giggles while reading the headlines; day-to-day history must seem amusing at his age. A young laborer badgers an aging miner with questions about strikes of old. The gendarmes went from door to door, but we fled to the mountains, where we roasted deer and read Karl Marx aloud; too bad you people don't read him any more. If you got used to working in a mine, you wouldn't feel like being in the sun. In winter you couldn't stand the cold, and you'd get a sunstroke in the summer. But if he could start all over again, he wouldn't be a miner. When he starts getting weak, they treat him like dirt. For fifteen years they've been telling him his silicosis was not getting any worse, even though it was; his eyes get so brown sometimes, his wife is horrified. But the doctor says what he wants to, what he gets paid for. A hunchbacked young man in a tight-fitting jacket goes up to two melonlike breasts and offers them a sublet. The woman, clad in work clothes, bursts out laughing. For a night? No, forever, says the hunchback seriously. As long as you desire to stay. And how many rooms do you have? The hunchback is trembling but is telling the truth: one. Any skin disease? the girl asks. No. A television set? That I have, and brand-name china on the shelf. I'll look around some more, but give me your address anyway. And if you find another place, I won't see you again? Look, I walk on the street, so do you. The hunchback is about to cry but keeps searching his pockets for a piece of paper. The girl stares at him. You know what? Don't give me your address.

Sitting on the benches all around are people who wait

between two trains, between faded orders and fresh slanders, midpoint between two women's merging sobs, between closed, crowded, dictatorial buses and private homes, between a cutting machine and a wife who is waiting at the station with two hoes; between the tusks of an excavator and a wife ironing a child's shirt, between a paternal foreman and a paternal presiding officer, between hamburgers gulped down standing up and the serialized nuptials of fairy-queen and killer-king; between a friend who has doubled over frightfully and is showing off his medical reports and a father wandering about with his iron-tipped walking stick, repeating once more at the beginning of the month: I know, my son, you need money, too; between the *Internationale* and the forty-second Psalm, between snowfall melting into slush and the white nose of a corpse. Between the sound of a church organ and the grin of a pig singed by a blow torch. Between the withering messages of a loudspeaker that greets the prisoner-of-war trains of the mind and the yellow-tiled, windowless room of recurring dreams, which has only an overlighted bed in it and a TV camera on the ceiling. Oh, how long people must wait on these benches between two trains.

Hesitant strategies keep my fellow citizens here indefinitely. (On some of the seats there are painted signs: RESERVED.) They are the professionals of waiting; from the rude awakening of early morning to lights-out time they wait. Lying prostrate on the floor they wait. For a summer vacation, for Christmas, the flu, a revolution, the lottery prize, the end of the world, a nervous breakdown, the burning bush, physical-spiritual rape. For an event, for something. Let an unknown bureaucrat locate my file and write on it: Your request is hereby granted. Let a committee visit me and prepare a report on my present state of affairs, and let them pay tribute to the work I have been doing all these years; and let me, upon hearing my name, step on the red carpet and have a gold star pinned on my best jacket, in the frayed folds of which I wear death ever more conspicuously. After a greedily devoured supper when I have already surrendered to the TV commentators, let the telephone wake me: I got the job, now I can really show them. Let them print my name in the local, national, world press, in a prominent spot, on Sunday, without typographical error; and on Monday let my fellow workers smile at me, a little surprised. Let someone with a view toward marriage lean out of the window of a personal column, and let him be called Barnaby and let her be called Barbara; let her have slanted eyes, but if she is harelipped, I'll be just as glad. Let her favorite color be blood-red, olive-green, or some other. In the winter let her bring me roasted chestnuts; in the summer let her tell me: The nights are getting longer, my sweet. Let them keep my wearisome spouse in the mental hospital. At home she is the red empress, and we must kneel before her. We eat spuds; she eats steak. The tables, the curtains, the walls are all red, and every night she receives us in audience. We keep beating her, and she keeps beating us, but it's no use—court etiquette must be respected. The door opens, she puts down her threadbare briefcase and puts on her velvet robe. This is her life; she is the red empress.

People wait for so many things on these benches. For their gall-bladder attack, and the sweltering heat, to pass; for someone willing to exchange his seven-room house in the suburbs for their two-room flat overlooking a yard. For the boss to retire so the promotion to department head could finally come through; for their husbands to go out of town so they could spend an entire day with a man in a borrowed apartment, where, in a darkened crevice of their daily routine, love-making is a little better, a little different. And they wait for their lover to become a widower so they wouldn't have to see his embarrassment when he says hello to an acquaintance on the street; and for that boy to sit next to them on the bus, whom they left that night with legs wobbling but who gave them a fake telephone number. And they wait for grandmother to die in the old-age home so they could go boating on Sundays or, in the winter, take a nap after a rich meal; and for the scaffolding to be dismantled in front of their window so the neighbor's idiot boy won't peek through the beams, and after a few cold spring days the sun could shine through again. They wait for their ancient enemy, who zeroes in on everything, to miss the mark for once; and for the day when they can enter a barracks with a roast chicken in their bag and see a person sit down on the other side of the trestle table, who at home would gladly listen to their stories of what happened during the day, but here there is nothing to tell. To kiss him would mean trouble, but it's all right to watch him eat *his* piece of chicken and glance back just as inquisitively after clearing away the bones. They all wait for an age of change, for the day when whatever is painfully missed now will no longer be important, when only naked existence will be important, which lacks nothing except perhaps itself.

Loaded down with bags and propped up by a cane, a triangular old woman appears in the square before the railroad station. Her yellow scalp looks pink in the sun, her shoulders creak; with the cane she adjusts her hat, which is about to fall off, exposing a pagodalike hairdo. She keeps moving the dentures in her mouth, which goes on mumbling dutifully even in the absence of listeners. A forest of pigeons, as dense as rock, descends on her. They lay their bobbing heads on her palm, knock on her paper bags with their beaks, a whole flock of her feathered friends trail her to the bench where she scatters her seeds—a proud tiller of the soil on mossy granite. It was worth staying on her feet for this moment; a fat halo whirls around her smile. Those souls who have temporarily assumed the bodies of pigeons not only tolerate but also miss her when she returns to a flat whose stale air could provide a burglar only with a dry crust of loneliness. She expects no gratitude; she has done her bit and has all but forgotten everything. The little she does know she finds too tiring to recall. She must drag time's tumbrel between the milestones of care, and has a hard time pulling out her shoes from her sinking footprints. Take it back, O Lord; I've had so much of what is just a little more than nothing and what can therefore never be too horrible to be beautiful. Improvement, change—humble words for good—are not for her. She eagerly offered herself to the vampires of love, obeying stern messages inscribed on open-air frescoes. They all wanted something different from her, some sort of service, some form of praise. The more she cringed, the more imperiously they gave their orders. It was a holiday if they answered her questions, which were silenced by her fears. The small stock of years was depleted; now each day she is alive adds to her guilt. Vinegar and dust are her only possessions. They have stripped her of all the errors of youth, which likes to see in each new day a nuptial bed. Nothing was hers except her ankles, which were clutched by canal diggers rising out of a deep ditch, and her look, which young and old drank in as they might a glass of red wine in an open-air tavern. She should have moved to another place where time has a stronger current and even she would have been noticed. But then she realized she would like to yield to the dissector's knife on native ground. Here even strawberries taste different and insults are cozy. This crumbling domain gives depth to every motion; here judge and criminal look toward the same salvation. She went abroad for a year to visit her son. When she returned she noticed how oddly small the station was, how the town square had shrunk, and how patiently the relatives, who had been nursing fossilized grudges, squeezed drops of false hope from stale bits of news. But when she said that the street lights were kind of dim, they turned away from her—self-hate has its limits, after all—and forgave her only when she borrowed money for firewood. Abroad, and for a while at home, she lied gingerly; it was nice to know that her hat, her mood, all her knowledge, blended in with her surroundings. Communal lies protect you from the cold; death far away is a hatchet blow, at home a falling snowflake. The seeds are gone; an old man with crooked lips watches her as she collects her things. The curator of memory makes sure they don't recognize each other's plundered faces. Although she would love to see a movie, she goes to funerals, and indifferently elbows her way to the sneering water-fountain that rises above the bones of successive cultures. The spout threatens to shoot mud in her eye. She stops in front of the church and waits patiently for the apostles. When the clock strikes, the broken-nosed, waddling figures creak reliably. She smiles back at their bowing and scraping. The meeting cannot last very long; they shut themselves back in the tower wall, and she is swallowed up by the shade.

The house I have been left alone in has survived my tough
family. The knots in the floor boards bulge, the softer
material thinned out under the waxing brush of kneeling
servants and the comings and goings of four generations.
After so many unsuspecting forebears, the boards will most
likely give way under my weight, too. With soiled feet I
make off for eternity through the French windows. I do not
like this house, for it was arrogance that made it so solid.
After a long day's work, humiliated faces watched from the
dark, motionless garden the elongated shadows on the terrace. When someone was thirsty on this terrace, for a hundred years he reached for the bell rather than the pitcher.
Naturally, not even a splinter hit it during the war: divi-

THREE

sional staffs moved in, aides-de-camp took off in a cloud of dust. Bear-legged generals threw their gilt-edged caps on these hooks. From behind my father's desk they ordered five, ten thousand of one another's soldiers to the casualty lists. After the generals' departure, my mother, like a cheerless autumn rain, cleaned with a wet cloth the outmoded globe rotating in a wrought-iron frame and standing under the antlers of a gray-browed stag that had been shot by my great-grandfather. I set down in front of me the iron head dug up in the cellar. Protruding chin, deep-set eye sockets —the twin features of a slow obsession, which are now my own. Cunning country builders: somebody is making a fool of us. In the lockable diary of blasphemous oaths, I find the vanity of vanities: quarrels, futile shouting matches with drunken, greedy artisans and sluggish workers who would steal your eyes out of their orbits. Like cockroaches in bread, pieces of charcoal were baked into bricks by gypsy bricklayers. For his massive walls my great-grandfather selected the bricks himself, testing them for a steely ring with a hammer. He toppled over rooftrees with a long-handled ax, and when it came to lifting or crushing stone, he outdid his day laborers. Even a horse is afraid of a master who builds so ruthlessly; only once did it throw him, after it had just been foddered and bridled, whereupon he tied it to a nice-sized oak and with his bony fists began beating it, but only its cheeks and its nose, so it could no longer bite down on the bit, or turn, or prance. God's plaything, he wrote of himself in his leather-bound book; in this abject world he strove for permanence. He rejected soaring arches and arrogant heights; the ground plan had to be square. In the courtyard the gables of the slightly sloping middle portico were set on stone pedestals that cannot be spanned by human arms. When I enter through the lattice gate and run my eyes over the unadorned masonry between six windows that loom green in the pale-yellow wall, I understand: he built for God. He praised Him with his abode; with Him alone did he have accounts to settle, and after a while not even with Him. But for many a year he acknowledged himself to be his Lord's subject. Foolish, straying, hateful is one who is his own ruler, he thought; a loathsome, stale creature is man, neither all flesh nor all spirit. There is incurable enmity between him and woman's body—enmity fueled by the emperor of death that climbs from star to star and whispers: Grain of dust, be your own master. My hatchet-faced, broomcorn-bearded great-grandfather reached out for his wife's cedar-bound commonplace book and next to her simple-minded sentence—Love compensates for all, but nothing compensates for love—he wrote: Hogwash. He didn't approve of her religion. Prayer is the elation before prostration, she wrote exultantly, to which he added with a growl: I stand straight before my Lord, like a stake. Later, when he led his family into his massive new home, with his wife on his right and his son on his left, my great-grandmother began to sallow. Death will soon pull my hands and feet from the stocks—that was her last entry, and she became a shadow before the fireplace. Then, one unnoticed afternoon, no one sat in the chair any more. Behind nailed-down shutters, in a rent cloak, my great-grandfather huddled on the floor from dawn to dusk, feuding with God and reaching for the empty armrest as though the long-nailed hand that used to clutch his beard were still there. On the wall of his forehead he hung up the engraved scenes of his marriage. Like a lamb on salt, a grown man fell on a lanky child-bride, sucking her breasts as if they were poppy capsules. In the chapel he was a carved head, but he became a mare egged on by the devil when, having deserted the failed revolution, he was given the terms of God's potent alliance. Two metal alms boxes, their keys gone, stood in silence for years until the turbulence in his mind and the conjuring patter of the late-winter rain resurrected my great-grandmother on the bedsheet of his closed consciousness. She is curtsying on the platter of a sunflower; near her thighs quick-moving moles bite one another furiously. She steps into the fireplace and jumps out as a pair of twins. The two of them are now combing his beard and, in mauve-colored robes, play a four-hand piece on the piano. Later the garden goes to seed; at the foot of the fountain covered with duckweed, white mushrooms glisten. My great-grand-father carves a dulcimer that is never to produce a sound. The eyes of Delilah holding her broken wrist over Samson's marble locks are covered with moss, settled by snails.

Meanwhile my mother is waterskiing in the sky, with the angel of resurrection, who is stronger than a motorboat, pulling the rope. He takes her up to the Big Dipper and beyond, among monkeys laughing on a Ferris wheel, and pie-throwing clowns, and lady circus-riders in red panties. For ten years she sat in front of the TV set, and for just as long kept wiping the dust from father's bronze head. The gentleman next door leaned out of his window on a pillow; for neuralgia he recommended camomile tea, for a heart condition, steambaths. He knew the schedule of trains by heart, although he never visited his daughter; perhaps she never invited him. Neither did my mother. There is such a thing as pride. Now this quiet English waltz and your little hat trimmed with lace make you blush, here, far away from the world, in the darkness of the air-raid shelter. In a chest of drawers I find my mother's Florentine water colors, above them my father's revolver wrapped in chamois, and underneath, locked up, out of my reach, a prophylactic. Even today I do not understand why he beamed when he came out of my mother's room in his red robe. At the bottom, unpronounceable names engraved in napkin rings wipe their lips in the earth.

A fox crouches under my bed, waiting for me to fall

asleep. It jumps on my chest and bites out my heart. A man with a sack stands in the doorway, and when I walk up the stairs he grabs my ankle and stuffs me into his sack. He sits on my mouth all the way home and later, sitting by his stove, eats hot noodles from my naked belly. Tal, the silk-legged one, steps out of the wall; if he tickles your palm with his feather brush you will itch all over and go on scratching for the rest of your life. Mother reads a novel on the terrace, the iron-legged telephone rings, she assures my father nothing is the matter. The japonica is in bloom, or is it the lilacs? One of us spilled the coffee and now has to change. What else can happen here on the hilltop? I play with my friends in the garden in front of her eyes. Close to the ground the archetypal events of human history are enacted. The shadows on the wall named *I* collide with the constantly broken rules of children's games; gushing sexuality with the ecstasies of the intellect. With a twig broom I keep beating the water pipe until it dies. I perform a balancing act on the fence, testing the tractability of space. From the top of the woodshed I launch my model airplane, and since it won't fly I would like to hurl myself after it. Now all ideas are wrinkled balloons, spleen lies spread out on the hot park-bench; I stand by the swing; ice cream melts in the sun. Why should I build the world's tallest building when they are sure to build an even taller one? Why should I run away to strange cities? People will one day desert them, too. God is taking a sunbath atop the woodstack. What am I to tell him? Somebody should be buried alive. When will it be time for lunch?

Great-grandfather's picture, in which he appears cross-eyed, hangs on the wall. His right hand rests on an ancient Bible, his left hand on the head of a Russian wolfhound. Three years after the death of his wife, in the tobacco shed, he shot himself in the eye with a tiny pistol encrusted with mother-of-pearl. Before laying him in a coffin, the doctor, obeying grandfather's orders, pierced his heart with a dagger. I follow grandfather on a small mountain-horse, drive a locomotive, cut up pine wood with a steam saw. Gypsies with hair and beards down to their waist are selling raspberries in cups; they don't frighten me any more. Standing over pigs that are gobbling their swill, the kitchenmaid rolls her eyes. Grandfather caught three trout in the stream, and in the evening roasted meat on an open fire. He collects wall clocks; there are several even in the foyer. None of them keeps the correct time, but he takes pleasure in them. Time the hunter showers his goatee and his pointy devil's ear with the pellets of diminishing minutes. At eighty he marries a chubby milliner who, upon their return from the honeymoon, raises her pinky when holding a coffee cup. But all is in vain; he dies of a stroke, and for a whole year after his death the dead clocks let their metal testicles hang in utter futility.

This woman with flowing hair excels at horse jumping; when crossing streams and fences she prods her stallion with tiny whispers. Wearing a diamond headdress in her braided black hair, and standing in the center of a *tableau vivant* arranged by the ladies of the Patronage Society, she becomes the winner of a beauty pageant. She dances in the roof garden of a hotel with a silver fox wrapped around her neck. In the curve of her knee the tower of the cathedral can be seen. She takes out her kittens in a baby carriage and eats pike perch in cream sauce to the strains of violin music. Five colonels goose-step around her table with flaming swords dipped in rum. If I hear her low, self-indulgent laughter, the ground becomes light under my feet. Even her perspiration smells sweet; there are no calluses on her soles, her small breasts appear pointy and firm in the triple mirror. But the speckled veil clouding her face does her no good on the promenade on Palm Sunday—she will never remarry. I preserved nine hair-raising chapters of her memoirs, which relate her numerous love affairs. She now lolls about and holds forth on a bed closed in with netting; the other inmates occasionally douse her with water. My governess squats in the bathtub with her legs crossed, washing her hair and letting the water run. I walk in; even the hair under her arm is soapy. Climbing into the tub with my clothes on, I grab her thigh, which is as hard as rock. She can't utter a sound, the soap stings her eyes. Terrified, she changes me quickly, but I nestle between her two breasts. In the morning she takes me to church; I promise everything. With my arm around her waist, I sit in her cinnamon smell. She keeps motioning me to pray, but to no avail—I reach again for her beautiful ass. I hide a toad under my sister's bed; when she plays the piano I twist the pedals. With a steel-wire dart I blind her white-ribboned likeness in oil. From the top of the cupboard I jump on her when she sleeps. I kiss her girl friend's ear. But when the bedspread changes into a lion on the back of the chair; when the fingers of a murderer slip through the slits of the loosely drawn blinds; when I press my face against the pillow and still must go on watching the picture show; when after swimming two miles I lie next to her on the hot pier; when on the top of the woodstack, under the acacia tree buzzing with bees, I feel like killing myself; when even the billy goat can't get a rise out of me with its horns; when it leaves me cold to see the rooster's head chopped off with an ax and its comb fluttering in the dust; when I accompany her to the station in a hansom cab, and she keeps waving her parasol from the train even past the semaphore, then I want only her. With her alone I want to skate, hand in hand, and with a wide sweep raise my leg to the sound of a Strauss waltz on the frozen duck-pond.

I watched this city from this window even during its years of legislative paranoia, even when the clerks of history were dispensing gas and bullets in behalf of the ferociously, mindlessly unified multitudes. The victims were left with nothing but their scapegoat costumes and their bleating astonishment. No one finds pleasure in their death, but the blessed, moronic routine of houses and gardens, the conversations between the green hillside and the long-distance-running centuries, swallowed up the temporary sobs. Everyday life-functions and catastrophes tended to avoid each other. On this flat roof, at the foot of the rusty lightning-rod, diapers dried in the sun. Their owners in the meantime turned on one another, or gave birth to new life, but on this rooftop, at the foot of the rusty lightning-rod, diapers still dry in the sun. Sitting on a small garden-bench, amid their cats and magnolias, old women are sunning their dry, barklike legs. For forty years they have worried that their families won't have enough money for their gravestones. They may well have worried: gravestones are expensive. In the end, though, these withered legs are devoured, under a coat of white marble and amid the uniform remains of woodpeckers and lizards, by anxiety- and magnolia-ripening, cat-rearing time. Standing in the entrance hall every morning, my father placed his cigar-smelling palm on my mother's face, and she kissed it when saying good-bye. On the day I received my draft notice she was fiddling with my belt in the same room. What is this? A bayonet, I said. Don't be a fool; I'll hide you. She passed her beautiful fingers over the bayonet's grooves. I put my hand on her mouth; she blushed and kissed it lightly. For two years I treasured this image; coming home from captivity I expected to see this face, but from behind the boarded-up glass door of the gardener's cottage an old woman emerged, in whom I slowly recognized my mother.

There is the clearing where, lying on our backs, we watched the resplendent geometry of a flying fortress, the firing line of the lead bomber's white smoke, the black pellets of direct hits. It was strange that ten thousand boys should be sitting in the sky, above the copperplate etching of a city that was defending itself with nothing but the din of sirens, and cellars smelling of cheese and wine. But when the masterpieces of warfare passed from a sky trembling with heat, and only scattered roof-slates remained, and the fresh cliffs of wrecked buildings, we were sorry the flawless air show was over. By evening we got tired of clearing away the rubble, and after nightfall, on the press shed's front porch covered with raffia mats, four girls and three boys, sticky from the wine we poured over our chests, tried to find out the limits of our bodies. In the cathedral of the October sunlight I realize there will be no grape harvest. Sitting on a millstone, amid drunken wasps, I am busy picking the red grapes of a separate peace. My friend's cap and boots and photograph rest on a wooden headboard. Between a sand pit and a shell hole a stone saint is shimmering in platinum light. Whether I survive it or not, this war is as absurd as all the others. I would like to drink, not fire a gun; there isn't an army I wouldn't desert. The terraced vineyards are surrounded by a stone rampart; an unknown hand has trained a creeping vine on a trellis, though it never pruned the plant. From under the tent of good will, from a perch on the press shed, I await the charge of foreign tanks. Their turrets pull to the side; the smell of open wine kegs, and of gunpowder, is wafted by the wind. The drunken infantry lies stretched out on the steep incline. For days the front writhes before my eyes and will not sweep over me. A chapel in winding sheets (the drill hall of four-hundred-year-old theological disputes) stands on the hilltop between overturned grave markers. A stray goat wanders in and out of the door. Behind the goat my cousin's lunatic battery advances—each of its bazooka shots is on target. I stumble toward him with raised hands, but instead of shooting me in the neck, he sits me down next to him in the trenches. Soldiers' honor erupts in flame throwers, even the vine-stakes are aglow. In the tanks the charred heads of Ukrainian soldiers shrink to the size of fists. There are other Ukrainians, sleeping off the heavy vapor of the muscatel. For each of their dead they would like to empty a cartridge into every one of us. If we decide to run, the Germans will shoot us from behind. But I can't surrender in the trenches, at every curve the attackers are clearing the path with hand grenades. I must reach the bunker and knock out my relative so we can wave a piece of footcloth or underpants from the tip of a bayonet. Before getting there, to make sure I will not have to kill later, I shoot a few Ukrainians, and can hardly remember the outline of their falling bodies. It's either they or I—a desperate situation. It was no conscious decision, but blind chance and technology, that set me down here. I only wanted to survive this war; and though my son and his friends may admire me precisely for this, and I myself may have human explanations for all the inhumanities, I belong to a generation of murderers. In the POW camp I had time enough to decide that the ethic of intelligent selfishness results in war, as does the ethic of nonviolent—and violent—love. Social reality is military reality, and philosophers are either clerks who would like to be colonels, or jailbirds who sooner or later shine sergeants' boots, or medics who are proud of never having been in combat.

It is as familiar to me as the punchline of a hackneyed joke; with its narrow windows, dirty green bars, senseless pillars, sooty brick facing, and skinny, disgusting chimneys, this Eastern European railroad station, as old as the century, has been pockmarked by the machine guns of armored trains and fighter planes, its partial reconstruction aided by slipshod saturation bombing. Troop trains pulled out of here in a magical uproar, often stretching to infinity the distance between waving handkerchiefs on the platform and shaved heads on the departing trains. Somewhat more quietly, the trains filled with Jews left the station on a dusty summer morning. Then only uniformed men stood on the platform, and lootable piles of packages—far too many considering the number of passengers and the available space in the cars. Later, much shorter, though no less crowded, trains brought back the lice-infested champions of jungle morality and chance, those who pulled through every barrage, who on their narrow barracks bunks washed the bloody excrement off their bodies, and for meat to go with their turnip pulled worms from the ground or denuded porcupines; who stood up on snowy roads even when it was no longer their feet but their memory that lifted them, who, while watching the yellow smoke of the crematoriums, suddenly straightened up; who would rather wheel their half-dead barracks-mates to the ovens than have them do the wheeling; who in order to avoid being killed became killers themselves—if nowhere else than in the steaming railroad cars where, standing naked, crushed, they drank one another's urine and were ready to choke to death and make a pile of those who were shrieking in agony as the guard on the roof of the train fired at them at random. On their way home they passed through the disinfecting station and the railroad's soup kitchen. Wearing striped pants and frayed fatigues, and clutching hand luggage of mysterious origin, they got into a horse-drawn cab at the stand which reeked of the dizzyingly familiar smell of hay and horse manure. The cab's leather seat was not much more battered than when they had left. In the soporific shell of the jerky seat and the clattering hoofs, they decided they had to can the film of their absence and bury it under the pavement of the present, if they wanted to equip themselves with the paraphernalia of a new historical era.

The railroad station was in a sorry state when I got home. Its tar-papered roof was supported by makeshift rafters; the paint flaked off the iron bars protecting burned-out windows. On a pile of bricks sorted out of the rubble, and on the armor-plated roof of a tank, vendors of pumpkin seeds and corn cakes were sitting. Peace was grubby and spellbinding. Stovepipes forced their way out of windows of wrecked houses, but the morning of the bombing, because it was over, became history and therefore ceased to exist, even though the flower boxes attached to window sills were in fact destroyed by fire; the explosion did cast a yellow pall over the granary of the United Aryan Wheat Merchants, and the menacingly good harvest of the last war year did crunch for two days on curled-up rails—the brisk, thieving poor could munch on bitter cakes until spring. All had been in vain: people from the waiting room crowding into the thin-roofed, makeshift bomb-shelter and blocking the stairway with their bundles; men pushing their way forward with their elbows and shoulders. The lights went out, and only calls in the dark tacked together families torn apart by subterranean terror. As through a biscuit tin, an eight-hundred-pound bomb tore through the roof and blew up in front of the ticket booth. For weeks afterward the people of the area, when they set out to exchange Sunday finery, or a mandolin, for some lard or crackling, used the scattered tickets, and as long as there were ticket collectors on trains and tracks for trains to run on, they kept on using them. But then the main stairway caved in; out of habit the screaming, bleary-eyed passengers still lifted their legs high, although they no longer had anywhere to go and could easily have stayed put—only by climbing across disabled, soft flesh could they make the journey from fear to verification of their own demise. Fathers, because they knew what it was all about, lifted their children over their heads, but it was no use: the next bomb fell right on the bomb shelter, mixing the bodies of the jittery ones, as well as the enlightened, with debris, to produce mortar of even consistency.

In the sky above the city heavy bombers went on with their choreography undisturbed, lighting up one by one oil and gas tanks in much the same way as world-weary commercial travelers turned on all the lamps in their hotel rooms near the station. In the light of distant flares, marking future targets, the inspectors of munitions works, holding their love for the night by the hand, rushed out to the square, along with the champion riders of the black market, deserters wandering about with forged papers, and investigators trying to track down the deserters. The previous night they were still dozing next to a glass of beer or playing billiards in an uncozy café where they dropped in after quitting another, even less inviting one, in search of beer, sleepiness, and billiards. But now one of them is dragging a woman still wrapped in her blanket, as if she were a rag doll. The night before, when setting the price, they took inflation into account. Leaning on the strawberry-colored marble tabletop, under the badly chipped, gilded wall fixture, she discovered interesting new things in him. Upstairs, behind the skeletal-framed blackout paper, while nervous black bugs jumped around the chamber pot, she drew his penis between her breasts. On her last night she wanted to offer him a little more. "If they check our papers, let's say we are together." The embers of their shared cigarette became the pulsing flare of a distant harbor; they escaped together from the hotel that sank to the ground. Cab horses, their manes on fire, were rushing toward them, trying to break loose from the flaming shaft bar. When their traces burned down, they stood on their hind legs between the scorching walls like the narcissistic thoroughbreds of the Spanish riding school.

In spacious rooms opening onto each other, under the reddest lanterns, crepes burning with the bluest flame, and questions clashing with the blackest force, expectant ladies and gentlemen clench their fists, exchange provincial dance steps and breaths, and let their nails slide down each other's spines. Hot flashes and liquid make-up fill their wrinkles. The drum solo of the cardiac chambers puts the gentlemen's high blood pressure out of mind; the loud-speaker cracks; stone is on fire; no pity for your toes. You take your friend's wife into your arms—she brings you cognac on her tongue. The friends you exchanged smiles with in the hall are now sleeping in the library of past perfect tense. The sets of clothes you see are shrouds, in each one there is a surrendered game. But your shirt is blood-red, and a conspirator hides inside, a wound-up sur-prise—only the person who puts her head on your shoulder at this moment knows anything about it. You kiss the part-ing in the middle of her skull—two quivers while leaning against the wall, you groan in surprise, a single window sheds light from a darkened façade. So long as you keep watching the light you are all right. You can recite your failures one more time and can write the curlicues of a poem under her navel. A deaf-mute whines in your throat, before uncrossable thresholds. You repeat the formulas of mercy—lies, all of them—but in the elevator you close your eyes, and when it stops on the right floor she is the one who makes faces behind the sliding door. Her shouts, her belly, her running toward your dumb lump on a darkened plat-form, free you of all charges: you can still hold on to her, she is still yours; there will be someone waiting for you between the time you wake up and the next meeting. But right now, in the rush hour of glasses and lips, between a slice of ham and a confession, a glass of vodka and self-denial, there is no reprieve, only the blinding light of an assassination attempt, the exclamation point of a massive attack. Now you are down to clasping the trunk of a walnut tree in the garden, where it will surely rain.

One guest would like to be different on this special

night; he listens to the secrets of wine-smelling mouths—secrets drawn from the expanded autobiography of humanity's collective memory. Inflamed by the howls of a rock hyena, kneeling, androgynous figures bow down before the horizontal flame of a candle. Girls in ass-length blond hair wrap him in silver foil as he rages and sprinkles baby powder on sabers and maces hanging on the wall. He prophesies victory for abstract societies, and then sees himself ice-skating in a pair of shiny eyes enlarged by hashish. In the meantime, his hot questions remain unanswered. Now he reads an herbal in the tower room. Recognizing a puffy hip amid tricolors and broken chandeliers, and hearing a double-voiced lament in the trimphant moment, he would like to make his presence known. But he does nothing and continues walking in the garden. White mounds are grappling behind the raspberry bushes; a woman pours lead for him: a sail presages a journey. Through curtains embroidered with lady acrobats and sea shells, he tumbles into an unfurnished room, where a decrepit colonel in a peaked cap wants to kiss him on the mouth and says he has been waiting for him; he bites into the rafter and thrusts out his behind. The guest asks where the toilet is and rinses the familiar figure of speech—the beam—out of his eyes. He clears all the tragic props off the stage of his private memories. On the sheet of dictatorial words there is scaly vaginal discharge; as long as it can be done, and there is someone to do it with, the sexual organs want to function. The fluttering sensation subsides; we have bright, family weather. A young mother enters the bathroom and thinks of her children. At the foot of the mountain, crisp clusters of grapes are on their way in seven trailer-trucks. Above flesh cooled down, glasses filled with cigarette stubs, sleeping and crying girls, birds begin to twitter. Temporary sound engineers turn down the volume on tape recorders, barefoot dancers, their foreheads touching, stand motionless on the dance floor. The rocking chair in the garden is already surrounded by the gladiolas of early-morning lucidity. Now we could tell one another darkly humorous tales of mine fields and prisoner-of-war camps. In this game we shuffle our pieces blindly between the common good and our conscience until we reach the next stalemate. With a tart omniscience we have overwhelmed one another with our pity. Asiatic servility and bloated Atlantic rationality—even our brains have been cut in half by the armistice line separating East and West. We mumble into our wine glasses that this is what makes us visionaries and frauds and anarcho-structuralists with prostate conditions, who are only good at celebratory speechmaking and sitting in judgment over friends, who, in enlightened self-interest, have already betrayed us, within the limits of moderation; though after a few drinks, for lack of something better to do, we once more embrace one another. We have already reviewed *ad nauseam* who knocked or flew over the crossbars of historical high-jumps. Somebody is again reminding us that he lords it over a thousand people; another can only recall his childhood nickname. Some discover a world of inert bliss in a clothes basket, and would like to immerse themselves in a steaming pool. No one darts across crunching gravel roads with swollen cockscomb; shrieks get caught in tree branches, memories roll under stacks of mowed grass. Under a receding, critical moon, the wind keeps tearing the dry rags of rebellion; shivering shawls gather for a glass of tea. On the parade ground of time, solemn promises march on. But there are those who know that as soon as they put down their glasses and try to stay home at night, cats with ringed tails will be whirling in their rooms.

Here comes Andrea, bejeweled; she has monstrous rings on each of her fingers, giant bands and chains around her neck. She drinks a bit, then eats; she only has a half hour. The clothes drop away from her large, brown flesh and small pubic mat. I can still taste the brandy on her tongue, the deodorant in her armpits. The sheet and my thighs are still cold, but on the spacious white of her eye, a dangerous black tanker has already edged away from the shore; in a moment it bursts into pieces, and the sea is covered with oil slicks. Before slitting the throat of a chicken, the Adventist, Annamaria, puts its beak into her mouth—at the moment I do not know which one of them is less dangerous. Pulling her skirt up to her waist, she leans out of the window, and I lean on her. Not even class distinction, or the blue velvet curtain, can come between us now; and while I ruffle the fuzzy down on her spine with my sulphur breath, she chants hymns in her throaty voice. Above the tree branches, in the clouds, God sees, knows, judges all. From the curtain up, the tearful Annamaria stands in heaven, from the curtain down, in hell. Aurelia hardly has breasts; her torso is long, like a trumpet solo. She steps over the potted palm, the organ—a hurdler lifting her humble feet through the air cushions of slow motion. At my chair she rolls herself up and places my palm on her head—she is now a silent, drowsy lock of hair. If I were to drop it in time, like a lost parasol it would unfurl toward infinity.

Over her broad, freckled back two strings of Japanese lanterns are turned on. If I had a fakir's flute and knew how to play, I would make her snakelike body rise in coils; now I merely twist her around my body and we roll down the hill until we reach an unknown ditch. Aurelia stands in her garter belt and is rubbing herself on a thick-furred bear; behind her back—one wonders why—are a whip and a rocking horse. The bear squeaks if her iron-ringed fingers squeeze it hard. But between her thighs and sinking breasts, which I hold up like a tired governess, there is that voracious bear. He is eating wild plums and sour cherries and blackberries off her legs and picks plover eggs out of her teeth. Amalia sits on a glowing rocking chair, and because she drinks nothing but red wine she bakes up crisp and tender. I can eat her from head to toe. But what the whip is doing there I still don't know.

In the corridor of the maternity ward I try to guess which one of the double row of infants behind the glass partition is my son. These beauty-contest winners, barons of Caesarean section, sweet ladies and gentlemen with glazed faces and amber brows, have survived the first ordeal —the real forceps and pincers are yet to come. It would not have hurt them to take lessons, while caught in the contracting muscle of a torn vulva, from those milling at the gate of the bathhouse of heaven. Or are they simply prune-faced old men? If their cells and the stars yielded the key with which we could unlock their peculiarities and their enigmatic, jagged handwriting, as they saw the air in front of them; if we knew more about them than what the tags on their little wrists reveal—our blood ties—would anything be different? We simply look at them, helplessly—inviolable bottled messages from the outer limits of non-being, leaflets from an airplane with unknown markings sailing into our garden, goldfish plopping into our water as we wash, gulps from a cup at a redwood table in a summer glade, full moons on our darkened skies, musical clocks of our destruction, soft explosives concealed between husband and wife in the nuptial bed, leeches on two luminous breasts, declarative sentences that cannot be contradicted, invitation slips to the sheet of oft-duplicated intercourse, rear admirals in full dress uniform and gilt-edged caps standing on the bridge of their cruiser and saluting a pier that is fast becoming empty, ice kings sitting in a sled with sails, their red robes vanishing under the seagulls before our eyes, caresses changing into bouquets of flowers on our smoothed-out hospital blankets, faces that can turn away from us as precisely as grace—how can we get to know one another?

I am taking him home from the hospital in a taxi; he is bundled up to his nose. My two arms are buttressed on either side by angels, while he wails in his queer voice. I bring home the grand duke of touchiness, a vomity tyrant, whose awakenings are witnessed by a houseful of people on tiptoes. He is a born conqueror whose damp and sticky paraphernalia overrun the apartment. An unpredictably angry, creaking, holy object, he is defended against me by every foolish crone. An insatiable striker, he doesn't want to eat or gain weight or grow teeth; I have no power over his tiny, devilish mechanisms. The moment we enter the house I know I have brought home my enemy, who will take away my woman and wrap himself in her flesh. A star and its satellite, the two revolve around each other—and I have no say in their love. Leaning over his light English bunting, I am content with simply being. I decipher his light substance: he is fine as he is—irregular, scarlet, careworn. I am getting acquainted with the character of a ten-day-old, with his quick, jerky gesturing and unexpected faces as he yawns, hiccups, snores, whines. His every sign of life is a burning bush right now. He fills out time, and his room, having been made meaningful, has the brightness of the manger; it justifies all that was and will be in this family. To pair off is a law of nature, to serve a single body a sweet liability. No one else matters, only he; others don't even have bodies. What bliss to be able to live the hours of separation *for* him, and to account one day for every moment. He is the smile of a waning golden age, a cheerful tablecloth spread over the molehills of our common future. Curling up in our cozy shelter, we consume each other, and our share of the broken pieces of our relative civilization. House rules are house blessings; the steady blinking of an eye reassures us; daily renewed contracts prove our existence. You are partnerless, so am I, so is our child—the melancholy product of our joint growths and joint demises—I shall amuse myself with him for a while. I brought home a boy whose narrow chest I can span with four fingers. I hold his hay-scented head under my nose and am terrified by our mutual defenselessness; under his impatient thighs I am but a humble whale. I brought home a crazy astronaut, a rooftop sleepwalker, rider of balcony rails, a noisy short-wave radio whose every newscast I listen to, but whose jests, boasts, and disavowals I will hardly remember on the day when, with a scissor jump, I shall leap out of a boxing ring smelling of sweaty feet, underarms, and intestines.

For a long time I forget him. He potters about, or screeches, at my side. I sit at my table in a dark room, and though it's I he is shouting after, I do not answer. I would like not to hear his voice. In strange hotel rooms I am so glad no one talks to me in the morning, no one sits on a pillow near my head, hoping to wake me up with whispers. As I cling to my studies, the barricade of unlearnable irregular verbs, I don't even remember the curve of his lips. Yes, I have a son, I say to a strange body, but this phrase makes sense only if I see him running toward me at the train station. The house is large enough; there is room for both of us. He stands in the balcony doorway against the whitening sun as detached as a catatonic. I look at him from the distance as he puts out roots in the world. His existence is a continuous adventure in understanding, and every person he meets is for him a flood of questions. I watch as people fall silent when he says something. His short guffaws and his drawings in the air are the physical residue of sketching solutions. His only reality is the future; he moves in a utopia while surrounded by the dusty objects of an antique shop. He dropped in here out of curiosity, touches a few things, laughs a little, and will return to the street and the store windows of fifty or a hundred years from now. He has the oil of the future in his pores and has shaken off the superstitions of the present. Foolish questions invite foolish answers, he says evasively. I am afraid he will tarry here just a little longer and then go someplace where subtler questions are asked.

The road was used by crusaders and adventurers, mendicants and cattlemen. Roman legionnaires laid its foundation with crushed stone, and now I connect it to a six-lane highway. In the subterranean chronicles of collective memory, I confront each new arrival. The plague came this way, and freedom; carts filled with eggs, marketers' wagons carrying calves, and machine gunners in armored cars who from their uncertain turrets shot at everything that moved; goggle-eyed messengers of peace came, extending their heretical mercy even to those who blinded them, and chapped-lipped interpreters of dreams, who urged the destruction of yokes and pillories. The wan and bitter preacher, even when pulled on the strappado, whispered: I have the Word. The pilgrims of risk poured into my city from this road, and in reply, black-blooded boys took to the road. The road: the bed of motion, an unrolled invitation to Solomon's wisdom; I would have stretched out on it forever. But I didn't dare leave the herd; I was fenced in by the city, the meeting place of roads growing drowsy under rows of poplar trees. My son will perhaps rectify the errors of a thousand-year-old settlement. Gusts of existence are still ahead of him, as well as the never-tiresome guessing games of the suicidal hereafter. Let him go before he sets fire to his father's house. The city wants to remain and the boy wants to go. If he is made to stay, he will dream of earthquakes.

I am going to seed. I open up the vacant rooms of the

house and send out my invitations. The secret doors are flung open, the curtains swept aside. From the gallery of my jealousies and the cold-storage plants of stern judgments come prancing out all those who have been nourishing me. They press their foreheads against stove tiles, glance back at me from the mirror, sit in my armchair, take hold of a glass, and launch, through me, a war of gentle terror. We fasten the cherry-red lanterns of folly on the poles of the intellect, stick a flower in every old woman's hair, a dead sparrow in every preacher's mouth. We graze the grass of change off one another's faces and guide our shivering hands toward one another. Everyone: feast on chestnut, which is softer than buried lovers, and on rooster blood, so you could crack the hardest trumpet. The rag of compassion washes the crystals of frozen laments off the walls; it wipes off the crooked letters of irreparable ruptures, the rationalization of self-love, the vapors of flesh moist from friction, the names of murderers whispered into pillows. Ride back and forth on rocking horses made of painted glass, bite off the fuzzy fruit of adolescence from the peach tree under your window, drop the minutes of family betrayals in the illuminated water of a fish tank, switch last wills and testaments—the names on them are interchangeable; rollerskate back into your past on the mercury drops of broken thermometers, heat up the unstained bandages of imagination; from behind the back panel of framed family photographs, lift out the it's-all-over letters, which you never really got over. Come, let's sit around the table of forgiveness.

I was a city planner in the early phase of socialism. From bourgeois I became a member of the intelligentsia, and was servant of law and order, agent of an open future, wizard of upward-soaring graphs, and self-hating hawker in an ideology shop, all in one. My father was a private planner, I was a planner employed by the state. To make decisions about others he needed money, I have my office. What makes others envy me, what enables me to run my fellow citizens' lives, what prompts me to imagine in arrogant moments that I am what I am, are wealth and power, and of these we both had more than our share.

I never hated my class. Having been brought up in it I was merely ashamed of it, even in its downfall. The guests

FOUR

in our house, gentlemen down to their fingertips even when muttering denunciations, knew precisely how long they could sulk before the crack of a dog-whip. To pull wool over clear eyes, to step on people's stomachs when they are pinned on the floor and gamble away their race horses' fodder; to rob one another when the chips are down, to requisition marching prisoners' backpacks, between two equally stupid alternatives to choose always the more expensive one, to record provincial precepts on de luxe parchment; at the crossroads of risk and debasement, after momentary indignation, to become debased; to answer figures with figures of speech, to call mass murders excesses, to dub one short interlude between two long betrayals a heroic age—these requirements of managerial fitness were by and large met. I was a party to self-delusions, if for no other reason than for being surprised that our satellite police state would rather decimate its own people than have others do it, and for respecting the stupidest defense of our peripheral interests—interests last represented in City Hall by a demented Fascist cobbler who passed death sentences by flipping a coin. Heads, he said, and didn't even listen to the rattle of the machine gun. They found cut-up women in his stove and moist hundred-dollar bills stuck to his soles, after a youngster pulled the riding boots off his writhing feet in the main square where he was hanged above an absent-minded crowd. Escaping the gun pits and prisoner-of-war trains after the bloody collapse, I didn't mind the nationalization of the family fortune. Lice and dysentery gnawed out of me all respect for the marriage between European culture and private property. I threw my entire mythology to the winds and cared little if the Persian rugs flew with it.

Blow up the gendarmerie barracks and let the prisoners go free. Allow miners into drawing rooms and foundlings in the officers club, exchange bracelets for baby food. Abolish frontiers, diplomas, ranks, private property, death sentences. Demand a right over public property for everyone; pulpits, platforms for anyone who will be listened to; print, sell without a permit anything written. Let us have city grants instead of taxes, schools instead of prisons. Turn city-states into national, continental states, devise a European system of planning. Self-government for neighborhoods and factories, grass-roots bureaucracy and civilian-controlled law enforcement. Let the city be a theater for the masses; let streets be avenues for free observations; let the child be guest in history's meeting grounds, for which we are all accountable. Let festivals be the intellect's conquests in the deserts of time. I knew little about the incestuous love between verbal illusions and belligerent self-love; I knew little about society. I stole back my body from accidental death, and was clothed in rags pulled off corpses, as I got out of a smuggler's car in my native town, slightly east of a Europe turned wild by her ideas. Until I grew accustomed again to celebrating my talents as ends in themselves, freedom for my brain was more important than freedom for my stomach and my genitals. For me the lesson learned from war was this: we must make the individual citizen less dependent on the state, and make the state more dependent on the individual. Later I realized that this demand leads to anarchy so I gave it up. Now I am ashamed of my realization.

I was not a revolutionary, although I shared others' impatience to leave my mark on the world, and participated in speeded-up metamorphoses of roles. In the ironic parable of history the intellectual plays a leading role. To master the world in theory, without practical power, is disadvantageous. We offer universal solutions in behalf of the dispossessed. Five phrases about the suggested world order could easily be learned. A promise, like God, is irrefutable. A new humanity's opportunities are guaranteed by the faith placed in them. Our ultimate goal is before us: a society of equality and unanimity. Ceiling frescoes depict no dissension, there is no strife between self-interest and ideal, when people are in the dark about their own goals. There are no poor, no suicides, no madmen, no one with infectious diseases, only a choir about salvation. Progress has no waste; knowledge plans, and rules; it recognizes and applies the law. Every event is purposeful; good and bad have set standards. Whoever joins up redeems himself. You can't have a toothache when you are marching. If you are not a traitor, in principle you are immortal, especially if you are at the head of the line.

We planners map out the future—what sort we do not yet know, but anyone who likes the future must like us. If they don't they must take the consequences. The future is a law, not a prediction. Let's plunge in; we'll find out later what it is like. The trumpet call of the cavalry charge always precedes the counting of the dead—the season of practical philosophies of history is at hand. The ax strikes, let the chips fall where they may. If your argument is meager, enrich it with a bullet. It is defeatism to ponder over the price you must pay for glowing tomorrows; the drill ground of history is leased by fighters, not merchants. In power, as in criticism, let us insist on purity of genres. For a revolutionary the only reality is reason-defying stubbornness. He is the voice-museum of blood feuds and fatigue, of self-justifications and grievances, of commemorative addresses and balance-sheet reports. Statesmanlike furrows around a drooping mouth; complaints about an unexercised body in a huge automobile; table-thumping, sobbing apology when dawn peers through a glass. A parting glance to the revolutionary: prison cell, hospital for heart diseases, retirement with honors, ideological battles in the veterans' old-age home, militia choir and brass band at a state funeral. The revolutionary always becomes obsolete, and he is always indispensable. He helps replace outgrown conflicts with new ones that he himself never counted on.

I, too, wanted to do some town planning, unimpeded if possible. The maze of competing individual interests has become a hindrance for me, as have squandered capital and the pettiness of planners and plots. I grew weary of the shabby town itself and its confusing spatial configurations, which reflected a stratified society. In it social and residential classes—from the marble-staired, baroque palaces of magnates near the town square, through middle-class apartment houses overembellished with mythological and botanical ornaments, to workers' settlements at the edge of town and gypsy mud-huts—were sinking steadily, transmitting the inequality of centuries to voluble materials. I rejected not only the hierarchy of the residents, but also the tyranny of enclosed spaces.

I wanted to cut through this resisting structure that let loose an ever-growing traffic on the overburdened town center, and build a new city in its place, in whose identical neighborhoods families, equal in social position, would no longer disdainfully keep apart. I was going to move vehicular traffic underground, break up the airless corridors of the streets, rehabilitate and turn into an uncrushable king the pedestrian. I meant to raise an earthbound culture to the firmament of the third dimension. In place of smokestacks begriming the sky and windowless factories filled with primeval machine-monsters, I devised an automated production line, to be placed under glass-and-aluminum domes. I would have liked to construct intricate children's towns in the loosened-up spaces, along with multipurpose houses with movable walls, and surround them with artificial lakes and parks. I wanted to see humming, expandable labyrinths around color-organs, in whose stylized side-nooks goods, ideas, language, fashion, ritual, and sensuous gifts would accrue and hold one captive. I wanted to build a great city, a provocatively flexible system of thickening time-spaces, biotechnical configurations of billowing and abating stimuli that would emerge—along superhighways, in cables, glass-tube tunnels, antennae, shafts, star clusters—from the carefully tended culture-landscape of pastures cared for by electric shepherds, year-round greenhouses, and plowlands tilled by remote-control machines. I did not yet know which of these technical utopias would be patronized by time, or whether these hill-cone-crater-spindle-pyramid cities with their spiraling population densities would ever come into being; whether we could attach to their core, on a radiating framework resembling moving tree branches, interchangeable dwelling cells made out of interchangeable synthetic units of space, or build bubbles of privacy above woods and parks. Nor did I know if we would be riding in air-cushioned tubes, automated electric-car-cassettes, on a city-wide network of aerial trams, or on multilane speedwalks; but I did believe that the new society would build a new city and would imprint its philosophy of history on the environment.

We wanted something we had never had before, and did something that was both new and old: we brought about early socialism. The armed forces were under our control. We couldn't be owners, only directors. Office furniture found its way into emptying apartment buildings—revolutionaries were now assuming their offices. We witnessed the pathos of haste: men with steely jaws, their shirts open at the collar, were kept awake through the nights by decrees about to be drafted. If the office is state-owned, then factories, shops, schools—everything and everyone must be state-owned, too. State shoes were more comfortable, state strawberries sweeter, state newspapers truer, state-supported children better. I myself—my pants, my diction, my inclinations, my conscience—was becoming state-owned, and a loyal socialist. As soon as it was taken over by the state, a dusty workshop was flooded in sunlight. A dusty teacher, when nationalized, pulled himself together: he was now teaching the new sons of the new order. The state is good; if the state owns everything, everything is good. Within a year happiness was all-pervasive; nationalizing was a breeze. I sit in one of the upper rows of a reviewing stand, under a potted palm and the leader's picture. The loudspeaker greets squalling peasant women delivering their quota of wheat in carts decked out with flags. Poets sing the praises of those who gave their all. Led by the roll of drums and brass band, uniformed children enter. They are grateful for being happy, and swear that their hearts beat for the state.

This was the golden age of lawmaking; the burden of decision was on us. The number of officials in my city increased tenfold in twenty years. The socialist state is a giant company headed by a state intellectual with or without college degree, but always appointed from above. After noblemen and burghers it was our turn to lash out at the horses of history. We abolished the prerogatives of family trees and family fortunes. Decision makers were going to be appointed from now on. We raised and pushed down hundreds of thousands of people—raised more than we pushed down. Those at the bottom for the most part stayed at the bottom, and those at the top for the most part stayed at the top. Although there was little room at the top, and the wrangling was greater after the change-over, many from the bottom held on. Twenty years ago one out of every twenty people was of noble birth; now one leader out of twenty is an intellectual. We choked off the traffic of time-honored privileges, prohibitions, passions, and hatreds. We decided collectively what was permitted and what was not. Those who learned this moved up on a stairway of desks. The law, and the lack of wealth, made us equals—the chief engineer and the watchman were both civil servants. I made decisions about sums running into the millions; he cordially greeted everyone entering the office, though he could have chosen not to. The whole country became a single community. We eliminated contradictions by fiat; harmony was preserved by law. We made plans in the name of public interest, and whoever offended us offended the state—which epitomized the very best in himself. Everything was interconnected; a line drawn with India ink on the blueprint constituted the building of socialism. Every turn of the machine was another brick in a wall that—the plan was clear—we had to keep on raising. It is nice to build, but it means giving up many things, and it's much more tiring when we don't know what we are building. But society is not a building; there is no blueprint, so perhaps the only thing being built is socialism itself. Socialism is what we live in; it is what was and is—not a goal, a disaster, an ideal, a law, or an aberration, but an East European present tense, a neatly proportioned order, an unfolding drama, the power play of interests, endowments, self-delusions and self-exposures, trials and failures. It is something we call by a name, something resembling us, though it could also be something else—the architects' philosophy of history, an article on exhibition in the museum of thought.

We don't know it but live it. We programmed a system and it programmed us. We traversed its logical probabilities as one would a network of roads. It is easier to see from within what we have created: a society of centralized reallocation, in which the larger half of the national income is distributed by bureaucrats, and where official decisions replace factional strife. The surroundings were unfriendly, and we, grimly determined. We wanted to win, not live. It was a life-and-death struggle for transcendence, and our only weapon was a militarily strong nation-state with a heavy industry that gave us both combines and armored

cars. A historical state of siege, a cold-war economy: death
to the marketplace, where it's no longer Cain and Abel
who barter, but two strangers from among their three and a
half billion progeny who need each other's goods and time.
Among men fighting over scanty goods, justice is to be
done not by the demon of a fluttering bluebird, or by
money rolling off government presses, but by a hierarchy of
virtues, whose only reflection is official super- and subordi-
nation. My work is not a commodity, but a foundation for
the future, a metaphysical service, a civic-military duty
backed by the threat of imprisonment. I receive in return
not what I can extort, but only what the state provides for
me. According to my superiors this should cover my basic
needs. I recognize in these men my spiritual mentors, who
preach self-restraint from the altar of industrial-military ac-
cumulation. The renewal of the city had to be postponed.
The pockmarks of war on the walls of our houses were
blackened by the fumes of a wheezing iron furnace. I built
numerous small concrete domes along the southern border.
Two soldiers with their feet buried in the ground could fit
under each, and thrust out their guns through a horizontal
slit. Today the empty bunker lids get in the farmers' way.
Since they are bulletproof they blunt the point of a pickax.
Cranes were used to haul them in a pile. They will be here
a hundred years from now—monuments to planned reallocation.

I became a technician of a centrally prescribed military
strategy, at middle level in the pyramid of decision making.
Placing my pencil on the blueprint of my people's future
happiness, and eager to sketch out the most daring visions
of our collective history, I considered each opposition an
error that stemmed not from the structural flaws of power
but from the fallibility of its executors. Like others, I considered administrative violence a historical necessity. I repeated boldface slogans from a few paperback pamphlets,

and when facing recalcitrant and selfish people, I was the law itself. The Plan for me was not an exercise of power but a means of bringing about the common good. I believed the military model of organization to be most effective: a single nucleus, tiers of downward-reaching decisions, which are carried out by lower agencies promptly, precisely. Reports going upward from below; orders traveling downward from above. Low-level interests are conditional and partial; high-level interests are unconditional and universal. We faced an underdeveloped society like generals who with their field glasses scrutinize the latest enemy provocation on a neighboring hilltop. We substituted one-way power control for the mutual dependence of self-sufficient participants; and because we seized more power than we could live with, we turned from commanders into offended dreamers.

I never liked, and brought suit against, notorious reality. Summoned before the tribunal of ideology, it couldn't hold its own: it had to yield. I believed that statistical surveys created anarchy, for they prevented the summary expropriation of reality. They were like the nervous father who would like to keep an eye even on the inner happenings of the nine months between impregnation and birth. Like our physicist colleagues who declared in a joint resolution that the earth was not expanding, we substituted sealed resolutions for a painstaking description of probabilities. I exchanged the ballot box for the military review, and ambiguous facts for planners' unambiguous ideas, a reality reflecting the offended mind for a reality boasting of the victorious mind. In the manner of a moralist, I dissected related virtues and errors, and attributed reality to my either jubilant or wrathful mood. I liked the first person plural. Looking down, I was we; looking up, I was I. If I contain in me the entire state, then my stupidities become risk-free state errors.

In exchange for the family firm, I became the head of a vast national enterprise. My father had twenty suits of clothes. I only had two. He had several dozen men working under him; I gave orders to thousands, including convicts in striped clothes, and said, I'll send over a hundred trucks —as though they were really mine. I built an ironworks, a bridge, a military fortification. Orders uttered by uncertain bureaucrats issued from the iron law of progress. It wasn't elderly public officials I was cheering with rhythmic applause, but the interpreters of my fate. Unity was more precious than the challenge of the mind. Any resistance on my part was not merely a slip of the brain, but the bad faith of a bourgeois. The sin of my origin kept infecting me until my identification with the state left no gaps. I existed for the state and did not belong to myself. I banished from my memory even the spirit of my imprisoned friend. Social transformation needs a dictatorship, which must rely on police power. I have to love this new order even if it stabs me from all sides. And if it takes me to task for some reason, I accept its verdict as part of my true life story. While drunk, I bawled out a friend in a bar: Terror is history's sacrificial rite. Really? he said, and left. I went over the logic of this statement several times, and because the chain of eventualities from theory to a gash in the head was inexorable, I felt terribly alone.

Even peace couldn't block the infantry weapons out of my fantasies. The guards dismissed us with an inane hit-tune, which I find myself humming even today. Four flash-lights woke me from my sleep; four outgrown, ready-made suits stood around my bed. It was quite unpleasant having to jump off a desk with swollen feet. And my loins were never so painfully sensitive as when I sat in the urologist's chair with my shirt rolled up and pantless. But I couldn't very well take home the blueprint of the underground airport, on whose construction six hundred convicts were working, all of them under me. I wasn't sorry this project was left unfinished.

We planners made nice company for one another in prison. Our attempts to guard state secrets lying about on the drawing boards were aided by numerous knobless doors. While munching on the sweetish meat of pigs injected with experimental serum, I had time to reduce my thoughts to a few basic formulas. I got as far as the misery of alienation—a dread of contests and opportunities, and an offensively defensive, prophetic-professorial-military aversion to a reality that devours the domains of the mind, instead of aiding its work. Among the older jailers I came across many adherents of meditative philosophy. The younger ones preferred the wisdom of action. They agreed that the world had to be changed; but for them we were the world, so I was drawn more to the skepticism of the older generation, though, according to them, the executioner was the greatest skeptic of all. I remained for another ten years an eclectic believer in authoritarian rule, even as I was looking at the gray, windowless prison wall from the outside (a prison wall built by my father, according to the prison specifications of his day, and for the most dangerous prisoners), while cowering at a marble-topped table in a sleepy pastry shop, in my dusty suit, before a cup of coffee, putting an end within a half hour to an undoubtedly instructive, and in retrospect increasingly benign-seeming, period of my life. After all this, between the laws of progress and the staircase on which we ran up and down at one time, trying in vain to keep the younger guards from patterning a bloodshot net on our backs with their pistol-whipping—between theoretical assumptions and improbable, though still performable, technical procedures, the pathos of inevitability melted away.

Dream and memory are ignorant of the passage of time. The city's decorated chief architect often escapes at night.

A compassionate dancing instructor abducts me through steaming pigsties and dim sheds, but in the end he always leads me to the examining officer. I say my name, who my father and mother were, the long number of my identification paper. I run along a tree-lined alley, in a milky haze. A pursuing car, its siren howling, cuts in front of me. Two young men with armbands kick me on the gravel path of a playground and stuff sod in my mouth. I wrench myself free and clatter across strange poultry farms and scrap yards covered with sheaves of metal shavings; but they catch up with me again. I continue running down a windowless concrete corridor. The flame of my match illuminates skulls in helmets, charred shinbones, a pair of glasses stuck between the blackened remains of fingers, rubber dwarfs dissolving in a blistery gas-mask case. Rough, mossy crusts of smoke cling to the walls. I carelessly step out onto the shore of an underground lake. A silver window opens up before my striped jacket and my groping fingers. Two young men sit in a boat behind battery-operated searchlights. One of them shoots in the air, and the dark echo chamber repeats the shot exactly four times. In the fine company of gray and balding gentlemen whose accumulated prison years make up a patriarch's life, a scandal always becomes an anecdote; our sentences are turned on the lathe of repetition. We tell one another cheerful stories, while missed youth draws the men's wizened faces into its halo. Only the one who is not here, who can't tell us tales, looks back grimly. The guards of oblivion take him away in chains, and after letting out a whistle in the corner of some corridor, he disappears.

If God, whose other name is Plan, resides in man, then the planner is the most manlike man; and whatever is unplanned comes from the Devil. But the planner subverts God by leading man into time. God has the secret of time, and so long as man is with God, he lives outside of time. He doesn't plan or choose or multiply, he only fulfills—humbly, idiotically, happily—the Almighty's plan. But as soon as he understands His orders, he comes to know irony and death. Faced with his own and his universe's limits, he turns from living entity into an adventure—an unhappy crevice nestled between plan and death. In order to substitute himself for the image of God, he turns his misery into boldness, and accepts the anxieties of the Creator, who,

because He forever changes things, has to cope with His own reluctance. If He were really almighty, He would be forever reaching His goals, and would not have to attain infinity through matter. His desperation is betrayed by His works: He has to share His rule with Lucifer, who possesses black knowledge, who reminds Him of His errors, and of the havoc wreaked by His runaway creations. He has to beget the Devil to be able to destroy Himself through him.

I plan; therefore I am. I feel my way in the world with plans. With each line drawn on the blueprint, I cut through the face of doubt. I can become overconfident, though, and must therefore guard against the all-consuming power of my plans. I should take lessons from Lucifer, the master of relative odds, who will show me the broken fingers of time, decay, and love, and teach me to laugh at my fear of One who refrains even from identifying Himself. Assuming reality—even if only in a name—is humiliating. Opening the window of my cramped, constant world to let in time, I try to figure out who is scratching and whining in this dark room. I bite into a fleshy apple and recall: the Plan is antisex; sex is anti-Plan. Wandering amid bodies, I feel in me the will to will not, and with my back to the future, I grapple with the golden haze of the present. God resents me but can't say it when He initiates me into His Plan, though He does place the jumping board of my death in front of me, and lets me know through Lucifer that He is uncertain about His decisions, and at the appointed hour He, too, will stretch out lifeless in the void along with all His works. He no longer wants me to believe that I have come from somewhere, am going somewhere; that someone wanted me, is waiting for me. He locked me in an out-house, there to peek at eternity through a crack in the boards, and try to shed my stinking flesh in a place I could never reach. Between bouts of despair and moments of clear vision—just to help me pull myself together—He taught me the masturbatory rituals of ideologies, knowing that to protect my goals, my longings, my despair, I will one day hire policemen and priests. He knew, too, that at times I must burn down the churches and the police stations.

I would serve Him, my impudently exaggerated mirror image, which I completed with what passed before me and will happen after me, with what is missing in me. After all, a lamp, too, is happy only when it burns. But I would want Him to demand that I liberate myself for Him, and suffer for Him for a lifetime. It is easy to think about (though harder to practice) settling down in nothingness, not wanting to be redeemed, being enamored of finitude. How good it would be to imagine that in the latrine of the here and now, God is the name of my freedom: He is that nothing which is not yet here, which I can bring to life and renounce for future nothings. But to love an absence with which no contact is possible via idols and bishops who feed on my own misery? To serve this less-than-mighty, universal sucker, this whimpering builder whose tumble-down walls are wrecked inanely each night by his drunken, refractory bricklayer. To respect an aging father, my shrinking co-tenant in the universe, who no longer interferes with my insanities and lets me repeat my disasters, who is incapable of uttering anything except vague promises about the hereafter. When I get tired of aping Him, He says, I could return to the garden where origin and completion are one, where time does not exist, where the idiots of grace wander about without plan or death. Having separated my work from my reward, He can no longer be my all-powerful Father. I might as well adopt Him as my son and mimic terror when He threatens not to bake me a sand cake. Vociferously I attend to my affairs; I may not even notice His demise. I could be longing for my mother, even in Him. Let Him receive me back in His belly. After illness, decline, shame, let Him regain His power over me as I take cover in His age-worn lap, in His parodistic coddling.

My imagination is absorbed now by the historical intermediaries who sacrifice their lives, the heartbeat of cultures, for an ideal. Moses, the first planner, pleader, seer, and leader of his people, has God tell him what He plans to do with the rabble raging around the golden calf, and is not afraid to pick grimy, insolent slaves as experimental specimens and punish them in the name of an abstract law. He is God's sheepdog, wavering between his flock and the task he is charged with: one can't exist without the other, only a plan can create a community. If he stops yapping and making promises, they will run amok in the desert. An intellectual, a revolutionary, he stammers cryptically about Canaan, though he himself does not know where he is leading the rabble. Still, with his simple and unsurpassable commandments he binds them together. They shouldn't eat maggoty meat or squabble over one another's women or cattle. They should love, or at least not kill, one another. He fixes the exemplary hierarchy of knowledge and decisions for six thousand years. Aaron is the high priest, Joshua the general —two politicians are the planner's two hands. Long-range strategy is Moses's responsibility, as are plagues, drying up the sea, bringing forth water from the rock. His is the essential task: to imbue his untamed people with the Intangible who has to be forever rediscovered, who is not so He can be, who can be a camel, a sandstorm, the scarface of a leper; who offers a land that only the sons of the sons can enter, about whom it is enough to say: He is the One. He strips away all doubts to make Himself visible in all the world. Still, He is not the world but a single flash in any individual capable of dazzlement. But how could one unite a people with this enigma—a people on whose hungry and inattentive face even the Unnamable finds itself bored. Moses has to lie, improvise, lead them on about armies, and bind them with his practical poetry. First the Plan exists for the Jews, then the Jews exist for the Plan; but who it was that Moses was talking to in the burning bush I do not know. In the hour of despair and frenzy every planner wants to be Moses.

I understand why Christ, the counterplanner, spoke cautiously about the gloomy dictator who planted priests and guards among the people and murdered his way through cities, offering bloody sacrifices to the jowls of animal gods. The proclaimer of the end of the world, Christ does not plan the city of the future for others; he steps out of the history of work and violence. He invites me to castrate myself for a heavenly realm that has neither king nor hangman, and that therefore exists nowhere but on an imploring face addressing God. Having rejected my weapons, I have to accept suicide by crucifixion, and the knowledge that I will not survive in tools, houses, and sons. Christ is the legend of guilt. He came so that I could have pangs of conscience. I call him a compromise redeemer: I am not assured of a paved road to salvation. He assumed human shape for me the same way any other resolute victim would whose cross binds me to the peculiarities of my race. No one revealed to me the meaning of my destiny; I became too old to believe in institutionalized redemptions, in the apostles and officers of historical timetables who receive from their superiors their truths along with their salaries. I became too old to be me—a planner. Christ warns us that he is invulnerable, for aside from being killed nothing can happen to him. His death falls only on those who took an active part in it. His freedom need not respect his uncertain conditions, for he can withdraw from his own self and give himself over to authority that cannot be rid of its identity. He warns: there are things besides this wavering adjustment, this greedy love, this obstinate identification with someone who is not even me. Love of life and its denial merge, as do meek presence and voluntary death, for a hopeless trip in outer space. Objective irony always had a window open toward sainthood.

But what can a planner do with the legend of guilt? I shot at people, and they shot back. Every kind of planning is an exercise of power, in favor of someone, against someone, or at times only for its own sake. I fornicated; I mourn. My presence here is an act of violence. As planner I see others as prisoners of their circumstances and absolve them of responsibility, though I cannot do the same for myself. I cannot be free of guilt, which is the price I pay for my freedom. There are as many moralities as there are relationships; there is not even such a thing as a city, only changing settings for self-preserving compulsions. But if I myself am the intersecting point of labyrinthine human relationships, this city is a far larger maze. As an architect, I can easily match the city's dense networks with my own. But rather than coordinating them, I subordinate the city's interests to mine. Because of my office my morality is more universal than that of my fellow citizens. If they offend me I am but a step away from passing a death sentence on them, though I happen not to be able to take that step. What am I to do with this shivering, incorporeal, all-too-forgiving, and therefore temptingly selfish love? It touches me but remains untouched itself. It can die for me, but living for it means rejecting others. His impersonal love—because he is without fear—can kill. Christ has to leave history when its laws are governed by the inquisitor, an exemplary planner.

The chief builder of a provincial town: there are better jobs in the world and worse. I wouldn't be a prison guard or a philosopher, although the difference between them is at times quite small. As planner I will remain between the two: a caricature of my own role. Here I stand among the planners of pyramids and cosmic cities in the historical queue, on the top floor of a ten-story building, amid the requisites of my position as chief engineer, in my carpeted room complete with padded doors, in front of a long conference table, to which I invite with a sweeping wave of the arm my coworkers, who come knocking on the door in order of their rank. By virtue of my numerous diplomas and academic degrees I preside at staff meetings. It is a modest share of power, but like a tiger to raw meat I grew accustomed to it over the years. The role is self-propelling; it carries me when I assume it. I wait until everyone quiets down; I smile all around and have nothing to say. How can a leading planner endure his workdays if he no longer wants to make decisions for others, and doesn't know any better what is good for them. He could of course yield to familiar self-justifications; after all, we long ago exchanged the coercive patterns of total political planning for the computerized mythology of balance-seeking, pragmatic planning, and classified the fact of economic growth as an ethical prerequisite that stipulates everything from technology to our daily agenda. The classic radicalism of official interference belongs to the past; it concluded a truce with officialdom's need for security. They would rather have the statistical bureau than the police checking up on the fulfillment of the plan. For many in my generation this plan-religion, which at first was refreshing, and only much later began to make others pay for its shortcomings, has faded into bittersweet memory. We are now experts on world dynamics, messengers of a future derived from the prolongation of the present, but we still keep shifting the weight of decisions from the uninitiated onto ourselves, and are not anxious to be confronted with independent, measurable control-machinery. With renunciatory solemnity we rule and allot, even when things proceed more smoothly without us. Were I to surround myself with the magic of omniscience, I would still be a puppet, and not the conductor, of progress. Far too often I confuse the convenience of intervention with the interest of the city. My egalitarian schemes were lame pretexts: we created a modified system of inequalities in place of older systems. The logic of planning with which I passed my time is not imperfect—it is unwarranted. The attendance sheet is signed by everyone; I open the board meeting. The plans are baffling, resembling neither the city nor us. The debates are no longer about the plans, but about the balance of power between the debaters. We have been working for three years on the city's thirty-year plan; as soon as it is finished we shall discard it. I grant a TV interview. Visions of the city's future. As predictions they are uncertain; as utopia, glum. I like neither the inhabitants nor the future itself. The reporter smiles, the producer signals with his finger that I have only two minutes left. I design one-and-a-half-room flats with coal-burning stoves for the poor, who crowd happily into them. The planners' flats are new, the bricklayers' are old. Whoever makes more money gets his apartment cheap; the one who makes less will have a shoddy and expensive one. Those on top get a larger share of what is in short supply; those on the bottom can write petitions and curry favor with the big shots. Where should the new housing project be built? Here a barracks would have to be torn down; we can't do it. There the rifle club shoots rabbits; but over yonder we just cut up a copse into lots for a mere pittance for the higher-ups. The expropriation fee will come to a tidy sum. It's far away, there is underground seepage, a double foundation is needed. By common consent that's where we will build. The new development will cost two billion, and considering it is one big compromise, its scale model looks rather good; the executive committee approves it in ten minutes. We are already at the door when one of us remembers that we need a statue: let's put it near the projected hotel, the reshuffling would only cost another hundred million. After a one-hour debate I find a worthier spot for the statue, which is sure to be clumsy and ponderous. Everyone is happy.

Which one of two villages should get state aid for school construction? The cooperatives in both pay interest and taxes; the men from both commute to factories in the city, and their taxes, according to salaries, are paid by the factories. In both the schools are falling apart; both need help from the top. It's also true that the president of the council in one village has excellent pear brandy, and the head of the farmers' cooperative in the other had an anglers' camp built for county officials. It's hard to make a decision: we can't leave it all up to the people concerned, for they might build schools in both villages, unscientifically, using their own money. A deputy minister was axed, as well as two section chiefs and numerous department heads. A number of high officials were revealed to have reached retirement age. An assistant director, who was a member of the inner circle, had already had one heart attack; he was afraid now of getting another. If he were dismissed, the fat woman editor working under him would no longer go to bed with him. You are not afraid, are you? I asked a janitor. I certainly am, he said with dignity.

The electric-eye elevator takes me up to the thirteenth floor roof garden of the hexagonal, metal-framed research institute. Champagne glasses in hand, we receive compliments on the successful design. Tomorrow the explanatory wave of my arm is on the front page of the local newspaper. We ravage the food pagodas decorated with truffles and goose liver. A banquet is the most sensuous union between the citizen and the state. The designers of pheasant and turkey edifices ironically serve public officials who have long forgotten the advantages of quick, stand-up receptions. The ruins of the beef Wellington provocatively illustrate my skeptical attitude toward my own planner's credo, which is embodied in inedible matter. Our stomachs at rest, we lean against the parapet and survey our works from the most up-to-date building of the industrial complex. Respectable ascensions at the beginning of a declining career; I pass the ball of my success to my colleagues, who return it to me. The grating liturgy of self-esteem and good manners: if I can't satisfy my vanity from time to time, it will turn me into a dullard.

I am beginning to inquire into the origins of my lust for power, and find my role as an intellectual more and more embarrassing. We are the key figures of a new age. National market, national state, national army—none of these could exist without us. Emperors needed us, as we needed them; we hated and missed each other. Later we threw away the costumes of courtiers and, contemptuous of rule by grocers, invented left- and right-wing romanticisms. The philosophies of planned states can be traced back to the guiding principles of utopias. We identified the state's interest with society's interest. We were the state, and exchanged the power of money for the power of the edict. We united dialectics and utopia; they were no longer an ethical alternative but reality's aspiration, incorporated in the structures of the state. We aim for a joint possession of knowledge and might; in a philosopher's state the planner is the minister. We speak up for doing away with privileges—professional expertise should be the sole qualification for leadership, and we are all certified experts. We need democracy until we get to the top. If history strives for the absolute rule of the planners, then any restraint on this striving is, in our eyes, regression. I would like to be more knowledgeable about the city dweller, but the more I know about him, the more he will be at the mercy of my paternal authority. Our critics wind up helping us: they can but suggest more flexible methods. The inner struggle of the intelligentsia is a contest between strategies of planning. Our power, as we grow more astute, becomes greater; from the national arena we rise unscathed to a universal sphere. We benefit from each change in the ideology; we can be communists, liberals, technocrats, or ecologists. Wherever systems become complex and the stakes risky, we become indispensable. We stopped being dreamers; computers now back us up. Prophecy became our prerogative. Little by little we cast aside the politicians; they can't start anything without us—we no longer need them.

Whatever we practiced with a clear conscience until now —even productive labor—has become dangerous. Our situation is precarious when by means of both war and peace we could abolish our culture. With each act we bump into the boundaries of our shrunken surroundings. We are no longer protected by nature's vast properties; when we make a move we confront one another, not nature. What was formerly self-regulated has become the task of planners. By extending our power over newer and newer processes, we have multiplied the need for regulations. Now, whether we believe in the religion of growth or in the theology of equilibrium, we must recognize that the planner has become more important than ever. We purchase our freedom with anxiety, and our security with the insecurity of our surroundings. Absolute power is the complete absence of power; by turning random events into law, we anoint chance as our king. The danger now resides in us, in our careless and violent structures. Self-criticism has at last become more important than criticism. Challenges multiply: we can no longer keep track of them. We must re-create our conflicts in more complex forms. The age of ironic reflections has arrived, but we are still the masters. Priests could be ignored, but not we, who proceed from earth to heaven, and are therefore not representatives of divine power. Strategic, biological, industrial, and city planners: by the end of this century we shall be the tyrants of the world.

I am learning to love the people under me. Without love I hate even myself. If I can't get along with those closest to me, how can I get along with an entire city? We are one another's sculptors: to live with human paradox is more adventurous than to create gods. If I don't want this city I can't want myself in it; I couldn't be any less scandalous than scandal itself. I watch a factory of inequality in me; the cunning beast is expanding, bit by bit he assumes power. He knocks down, sets up, lays claim—and can't even keep track of his conquests. Before breaking down into interchangeable parts he would like to prove that what he calls *I* exists, and is not simply a grammatical link between stray verbs. Any device—from violence to pathos— will suit him if it makes him indispensable. He always wants more for less, and because he is as stupid as his goals, he suffers from the responses of those around him. His eagerness is held in check not by morality or self-moderation, but by the voraciousness of others. He would blow up whoever stands in his way. If he is beaten, he longs for the future, which will be devoured by his achievements; they will be his even in death. His particular brand of humanism justifies everything he does; whoever wants something else is inhuman. Even the word God is an abbreviation for his boasts.

The soul is a balloon; like a chicken's belly it is filled with tiny pebbles. A few roll out during my peaceful hours, and it becomes lighter. Like a soap bubble from a straw, it passes lightly from my mouth into the void when I die. But for each pleasant hour I have so many that are not. I have reason to fear that my gravelly soul flutters between earth and sky, and I hold on to a man who is no more, a planner who has no plans, a shivering gap, a compulsive pebble-hoarder. He twists and turns his head like a scratching hen. In his excitement this round little fellow snaps up everything—worms, the Great Bear, a dictionary, a cathedral, even me. And when I say *I* it is he I could be thinking of.

The chief planner sits in his fragile armchair, prepared for the worst. He can consider proper only what his superiors will still find acceptable tomorrow; but because predictions are risky he makes them carefully, very carefully. The stakes are high, he can't be too friendly; either he reports or he is reported. What would he report, anyway? Besides what he has he wants very little. More power means more hurts; he has compassion for his former rivals, who tumbled out of the arena with the funeral wreaths of their honor. Those clumsy figures reeking of poverty have no more say in the contest of immortality. He was more clever, but now he would trample underfoot even their memory. His camouflage, his gray business suit, feels like his own skin; the so-called difference between the two he refers to the tribunal of seriousness. Humor is no sin, but fighting is serious business, and if you joke today, tomorrow you are likely to laugh in your superior's face. The planner prefers cool, dignified kindergartners who are quick to ostracize the impulsive spoilsport in their midst.

He knows that those coming after him can only strive for what he has more of and others less. After forty, every planner becomes ill if he hasn't yet been made department head. Whoever is left behind is not consoled by a philosophic mind, but is plagued by comparisons. What good is it to be division chief if one's old friend is already director general? Where will timeless values get us? Our only fixed point is the totem pole on which we feel we deserve a higher place. The bureaucrat is bound to his fellow workers by incurable resentment. He is afraid of those below him and those above, and would feel more secure if more people were working under his leadership—one more, a thousand more, ten million more. As a precaution he must always reprimand someone, the quiet one as well as the talker. (In the depth of his silence even a deaf-mute can be mocking.) A statement ought to be valid only if it corresponds with what he says.

Even though he is on top, those stirring below him anger him. In the end he is preoccupied only with insinuations and senile revenge. Everything he is told he misunderstands, and he replies in enigmatic commonplaces. He can recall only his hind thoughts and confuses even them. He has become so touchy he resolutely suffers from every word uttered around him until he proves it to be wicked nonsense. He begins to pick on various groups and blames his failures on them. Vague as he is in labeling them he knows precisely who belongs to which group. He is no longer *I*, but *we*. His words mean more than their definitions in a dictionary. Everything he does or doesn't do is a symbol, a parable, a ritual. Soon he will want to be seen even when not present, and be heard when not speaking. In the name of humanity, he hates the entire human race. He feels the time may have come to redo everything, and make it all resemble himself.

If the operation succeeds, he will be God, calm and infinite. But if he slips, the universe will be reduced to his own feces, with only an old-looking child whining over it.

An appointed eulogist, I stand between two iron pillars crowned by the flame of incense, and assure the deceased that he has done his best. I exaggerate my regret over his absence and promise to cherish his memory. Under the ivory-colored shroud lies my director's head, held together with wire. With his back to the window, which overlooked another company headquarters, he sat in his soundproof room. In the mirror he saw a high-echelon executive, who had been sitting successively in enough leather-upholstered swivel chairs to fill a showroom. He pushed his present chair close to the wall—a chair replaceable only with the tapestry-covered armchair of honorary presidents and other venerable corpses—leaned his left cheek against the

SIX

wall, and, with a light handgun that came with the job, shot through his left temple. The bullet pierced the wall and in the next room knocked over his thousandth cock pheasant, which was sitting on top of a safe covered with circulars and documents marked CONFIDENTIAL. (The bird's hot intestines had been replaced by ingenious plaster filling.) Five days ago he asked me grimly to press his stomach with my fingertips to see if it wasn't too hard. They called him, came for him, but he slipped away before the biopsy, the results of which—according to the autopsy report— would have been negative. He insisted on his suspicion; perhaps he wanted to identify that part of him which made him stop wanting to go wild-duck hunting on pear-brandy-smelling mornings, or ask me in the early afternoon, in a few tensely empty words, for the key to my apartment.

Thirty-two years in the movement. First come the tests of strength: he has to deliver a letter to a fake address. Were he to say he had done it, not even his girl friend would return his greeting. His pseudo-detective friends drag him into a car, blindfold him, and sit on his head. They stretch him on a pulley in a cellar, attach electrodes to his wrist and ankle, and slowly turn up the voltage. Still he wouldn't reveal the name of his contact. On the seventh day they embrace him. Death to the fascists, freedom for the masses; besides slogans nothing matters but the technical problems of carrying out orders. He stabs a German in the neck and steals his telescopic rifle. He buries himself in the limestone mountains of Bosnia and from his hide-out aims at the eyes of an approaching driver. Soldiers in pike-gray uniforms jump out of cars and trip on sliding rock amid blue shrubs. He watches from under a stone bridge the painful kolo dance of fellow partisans who are pulled along a rope. After a skirmish he drifts on the foaming water, nursing a shoulder wound and watching eyeless skulls rushing past on a curtain of water. A human column sinks into a room-sized hole cut by an explosion. He can no longer touch his deep-voiced lover, for he grabbed her traitorous father by the beard, shoved him into the hole, and stepped on his desperately clasping fingers. In the summer of '45 he comes home and parcels out land among the peasants. His telescopic rifle and his Gestapo identity card become the proud proof of our town's meager resistance efforts. He himself is arrested in 1949 for having once possessed a forged identity card. For five years the name of the Gestapo spy is mentioned only in whispers in our town.

With my funeral oration I breach etiquette. In front of the uninitiated I call certain facts by their name. As a result, the wide, sad faces of the mourners standing in the first row and linked by a special telephone line grow aloof. The man in the hearse shot himself to be rid of their company: when with them he hated himself. As requested by the official invitation, he pinned on all his medals for the anniversary celebration of the October Revolution; with every step he took he jangled louder than the smaller and fatter bureaucrats who were technically his superiors. At receptions he wasn't obliged to mix, and could shake more than the prescribed number of hands. Even his chauffeur was allowed to pass by the other personal drivers. For years he was the first man in the city; I thought him irremovable, but in coming to us, it seems, he was already shunted aside. At times he left his desk, at other times entire departments were abolished under his swivel chair. Since he was no longer afraid of being taken for a fool, he didn't label the wastefulness of high-level bunglers historical retribution; in between his failures and responsibilities he did not lower the iron curtain of the mighty *we*; on the stage of accumulated power he didn't enact the wretched drama of solitary responsibility. He did not spare his superiors; if they wanted peace of mind, they would have to be ready to pay the price: a privileged city poised between silence and eruption. Power diminishes if it doesn't increase; all it takes is technique, stamina, tough maneuvering, daily jockeying for position. But let's not push for it too hard: the trick is not to make decisions but decision makers; to stick to chosen paths, even if they are the wrong ones, as long as strategy follows rules and is not sheer frenzy. Whoever talks a lot is a necropolis of retracted ideas, setting his own traps with his contradictions. Decision making takes special skill; it could be emulated, practiced, but never learned from a manual. Whoever can't stand being dull will try to shine until struck down; whoever has no power will have to fight for it—he who has it will not give it up. This man thought of himself as a pragmatist, and was annoyed when I pointed out lapses in his pragmatism. He could have made it even bigger, but in an unguarded moment he disregarded his conservative instincts and threatened to resign when he could no longer be sure that they would beg him to stay. When he became my immediate superior, his career was on the decline. He read a few books and didn't hamper our work. He could now stand without the aid of his official title, and we, too, could stand up to him according to the relative stability of our position. The give-and-take between us had an almost festive air; it was April Fools' Day compared with the insipid memory of our previous directors.

My consciousness, like everyone else's, is continuous perception; it is memory and directive, but its program is closed, repetitive, unreal. Perhaps I want nothing beyond my remaining years; and because my doddering antifuture promises pseudo fulfillments only, I try to realize my potential in my profession. The higher my position, the more I exist; let others ask me instead of my asking them; I want to be feared rather than be fearful. I settle into this space, my role fills me out. As the floors get higher, the stakes get larger, and with them, of course, the chance of failure. But during the course of my systematic advancement, a pushy fellow in me is getting out of hand. His specialty is guerrilla warfare, devious stratagems to gain void-filling privileges. I want to be the one to write on documents: permission granted. When I pass through offices I want even those wishing me ill to rise. I should be able to hire people I need and retire those I don't. Committees should work around the clock on my ideas, and agents of my curiosity should keep computers humming until they come up with a verification of my hypotheses. I should smile even when I am tripped, and shouldn't hit back unless I know I can win. I should declare my rival's stupidity wisdom so that his inflated vanity can be an ally in my attempt to realign cliques and mollify ringleaders. I shouldn't be disturbed if an unrequested television set brought into my room starts crackling even when turned off, or if my secretary keeps leafing through my notebooks. I should be able to say, and make others endure, what is on everyone's mind. Ultimately, all I want is to loosen my bonds; to be free.

Yet I have to live in peace with the powers that be; they may not know it, but I am a resolute defender of their interests. Worn down by the general malady, they can be brainwashed into serving pseudo goals. I meet my presumed adversaries halfway; I sneak up on their hind thoughts. I fear them and they fear me; I mock them only as much as I mock myself. We should really come to terms before we choke one another to death. I am not insulted if my colleagues censure me for being secretive about my intentions, or if they wonder if I might be going senile. In their place I would share their resentment. Too many people take their cues from me in this town, where rodent-like cowardice and aggression are natural forms of behavior. I can't shorten the leaders' terms of apprenticeship; they must fend for themselves. I myself have learned well when to multiply my appearances in the public arena, and when to decline a dozen invitations. I have also learned when to leave everything, and shift the burden of a much-needed decision from an anonymous body of men to a single, defenseless bureaucrat's conscience. The higher-ups need me more than I need them; still, they could give me the sack at a moment's notice. I know my job, I am in my place, I can only do what I am in fact doing; yet the privileges that go with my position are not mine; they can always be taken away.

Since I am on the fringe and can easily be brushed aside, I am a serene representative of this city. A mayor, a judge, a police chief is sooner forgotten than the builder, whose houses remain. I observe the strategy of independence and surrender, the allies and enemies of my power. Aside from being right, I hold little sway over my fellow citizens, except perhaps in knowing that they, too, would like to be right. Since I am neither hero nor traitor, and am more aware of the absurdity of my situation than those who either flatter or curse me, I am not much interested in how I appear to others. I long for a death that is the end of life, not its interruption. As a member of the establishment I would like to feel better about my job. I am convinced that it is less disastrous to curtail the authority of official decision-makers than to cool the petty ecstasy of administrative interference. There isn't a duller way of discrediting the patient truths of the left, which have been in the making for a millennium, than to have intellectuals don military caps and make them line up and bark commands. The history of my city compels me to be disciplined. I do not give in that easily; when faced with small-time administrators I rely on my comedy routines: I tell jokes and resort to wiles. If I ask the right questions, even those who rage against me have to agree with me. Underground streams of thought are a potent force; I keep up the flow of questions. If a reasonable compromise presents itself, I content myself with it; if not, I must either retreat or fight. I am tired of being a disgruntled officer in a provincial garrison. If only as a therapeutic exercise, I would like to see the centralized reallocation of early socialism replaced by modern socialism's open, covenanted system of conflicts.

I am aided by a tradition that is several thousand years old. An intellectual in bureaucratic clothing, I am heir to all clever machinery, every open-ended question, every disavowal of superstition, and every tale in which mind triumphs over might and reason leads angry terror by the nose. I attempted to secularize religious axioms and abandon five thousand years of theology. At last we have gained a bit of freedom from God; it's time to examine—and let me be the first examinee—the dogma of humanism.

You are a technocrat, my son said; you think the alliance between knowledge and power is inevitable; hence the high-handed questions with which you measure errors against simplified answers. Your overstrained technical logic fetishizes achievement and economy; you say the city should be an inexpensive and efficient operation; the decisions made today should become routine implementations tomorrow. The worker, you say, is a continuation of the machine, the tenant of his flat, the pedestrian of the sidewalk. The difference between people should be great enough to enable them to compete, but not so great as to make the loser give up the fight. People should see themselves as goals, but they must also be the most economical tools in the hands of a society that has already surpassed them, and that must keep on advancing. For you, even rebellion occurs only to correct a malfunction in the system. Revolution is a limited-feedback operation; with rational controls it can be avoided. You shrink from extremes, from suffering that does not put itself in parentheses but accepts the risk of scandal; from any challenge that points beyond the increasingly complicated cycle you take to be the world. You do not understand my revulsion against the calm sport of adaptive rule-refining. According to you man does not act: language thinks for the speaker, the work process for the worker. You measure freedom as you might the length of the city sewer system; you would convert human relationships into a simple code. An actor, you say, must submit himself to an interpretation of the drama that transcends his role; a higher verdict is needed to put parts of a whole, struggling to go beyond their boundaries, in their place. From the vantage point of the whole, you view the parts condescendingly, and do not understand why I identify blindly with the part, accepting the probability of error and punishment, rejecting that which I cannot grasp with my reason.

Like a knife thrower he fenced me in with his verdict; in order to avoid arriving at a common denominator, we kept misunderstanding each other and ourselves. Yours is the distant future, I would say, mine is the past and perhaps a few more opportunities. Our truths are not interchangeable, our morals are different. But whatever we have, we should keep, and be held in check only by the demands of self-preservation and elementary courtesy. I do not for an instant say that I would gladly offer my place, coveted by many, to eager young competitors. Let them take it away if they can; if they can't let them sulk, snivel, and perfect their below-the-belt blows. I cannot conceive of giving up any of my privileges; I rationalize, rather than regret that history is a running battle between the promises of equality and the restoration of inequality. Instead of being filled with resignation, I want to be bold enough to turn criticism into self-criticism. I am a bureaucrat; I try to reconcile the demands of power with the presumed public good, and therefore need law and order. However, I also agree with the rebel: if the existing order is easy to overthrow, it deserves to be overthrown. But if you don't believe either in a change of the guard accompanied by the rattle of guns, or in bloodless competition, in which one needn't necessarily lose, since advertisement copy is less of a threat than an indictment, what else could you wish for but the elegies of self-satisfied good will, in a no man's land of the mind. Why should I alleviate the pain of my quickening death-throes with the color brochures of mercy? I am indeed an old man who, like those before me, finds consolation in the image of the new man who will be a stern interrogator or a nervous fool.

Bow the head: put a fatal stab here. If your father doesn't surrender, he must be laid low. Now no one stands in your way. You can eliminate the error that you feel you are, and be certain that you are also the attention aimed at your errors. You could open up your doors, fill your room with guests, and speed effortlessly toward precise destinations. Having outgrown my shadow, you now outgrow your own mirror image; your freedom returns you to me. But only if you sentence me to both life and death can I count on your forgiveness. I could help you, but let's face it: I don't allow myself to do it. Perhaps it amuses me to knock my son to the ground.

Builder and philosophy student; an apprentice planner in the department of city planning; a nurse's aide in the suicide division of the emergency ward; a theatrical promoter placed under police surveillance for dangerous vagrancy; a violent criminal sentenced to a six-month prison term for insulting an inspector. In prison, pathological fits of rage: he pulls his whip-brandishing prison guard from his horse and tramples him underfoot. Another mounted guard tries to drag him by his chained wrists toward the warden's office, but he pulls down this man, too, and beats him with clasped fists. Responding to an alarm whistle, three men come and remove him from his victim. He leaves maximum security with a facial twitch and visual disorders. He cannot hear commands, doesn't answer questions, and is finally transferred to a civilian hospital. During the first few days he wouldn't even talk to me; now he is willing to walk with me in the garden. Every other day he is in an insulin coma; I pay him daily visits. I did a three-year stretch; he is in for three months. My grandchild, if I am to have one, will probably be deprived, by historical progress, of an initiation into manhood. In front of a gas-mask factory, on the platform of a bullet-riddled ark in a boarded-up synagogue, on the rain-soaked open-air stage of a comic opera, and in the lounge of the mental hospital whose walls were filled with paintings of sea monsters and baby chicks, this subversive man of the theater insulted the basic institutions of practically every society with his bristling parables. Even the good-natured inmates wanted to have nothing to do with him. Now he is slowly coming to, and smacks his lips as he did twenty-two years ago under a rattle stretched out on a string.

I pushed him down; he stabbed me back. We missed and strangled each other; the more he agreed with me, the more he tried to expose me. The pressures of sentimentality: I wanted his freedom to be free of risks, so he became a paratrooper and a motorcycle-racer—a record breaker in stockpiling perils. He found it reassuring that I worried about him; had he been convinced that he would kill me with it, he would have considered suicide. Ill-suited to make friendly accommodations, he was a master of unpleasant situations. He always kept an insult in reserve, to which I replied with an even greater insult. When he was an adolescent I missed him less than he missed me. He had to overthrow my power, tear out the historical judgments implanted in him. I would have liked him to abandon the poetry of impotent omniscience, which is only a step away from the even more inane enunciations of triumphant reason. He wanted to hate with purity, and thus was no better than the one he hated. He spoke of alienation, but was craving power, just a tiny bit of power, then a little more. He would have liked to repent, to act, to strike: intellectuals are soldiers at heart. A teleological animal, he couldn't live with compulsions that made him feel worthless. Perhaps he was more persistently impatient than his contemporaries: he wanted to be himself, and it would have been useless to offer him the unceasing excitement of life and death. He can only be free if I am not; but even if I have no friends, it was I who built this city—either he blows it up, leaves it, or adds to it a little. But what should a kind-hearted boy do who hasn't yet learned to defend himself against all his mothers and fathers? He eagerly surveyed this city, the cathedral, the streetcar; I kept quiet so as not to mock his new-found enthusiasm. Actually, I liked his energy. I didn't really expect him to sit in my office, work a bit in the morning, belch a little after lunch, and jump up when the director dropped in. He wanted to break every record and invade the celestial or historical hereafter. Or he may only have longed to sit in a vanilla-smelling pastry shop where well-behaved guests ate their ice cream and biscuits to the sound of soft music.

A radical planner amid structures of clay—the knight of the luckless mind. Cutting into unbending realities, he wound up wounding himself. He knew that planning was an exercise of power, in favor of certain groups, against other groups, so he ended up suspecting his own motives. He hated statements about the public interest, detested the maudlin reconciliation of individual and societal interests, pondered over new spatial systems, and was bored at the prospect of designing a conventional office complex with a marble façade at age forty. He couldn't condone amateurish anarchy, the corrupt accidents of uncontrollable, militaristic overplanning—the giving away of useless rabbit-hutches, bought with everyone's money, with nobody's money, by officials, to their official-friends. In the end he remained a wiry intellectual, an adventurer among structures that surpassed his intelligence. He would have liked so much more power than could be attained that he would rather lay claim to none at all. Harboring self-hate, he embarked on a cave exploration amid the crocodiles of the unconscious.

He became a terrorist of interrogations; he turned informal inquiries and opinion polls into inquisitions, and infected his subjects with his own tortured and explosive helplessness. A university lecture and an interrogating room became a single seminar for him. Later he thought up a few slogans that I found interesting: Let the presumed presume their presumptions. Freedom is to be sought not in the rearrangement of institutions and restrictions, but in everyday practice, here and now. Realism is accepting what exists: whoever respects given reality will respect ossified laws. We received culture in order to supersede it, relieve it of its false values, and deprive it of its religious rationale. Reality begins beyond the boundaries of the possible; the only true realism is irony. The prisoner is freer than the warden because he is quicker to laugh at himself. Nothing is more disturbing than fear or self-justification. The best way to protect freedom is with a joke. Tyranny need not be dismantled, only disrobed. It should be encouraged to go beyond itself and uncover the absurd in its solemnity, the chaos in its order, the rules inherent in its errors, the rearranged inequalities in its acts of goodness. We can all help it spot metaphors in dogma, free choice in inevitability, paid-up taxes in gifts, the epigrams of self-interest in the odes of morality, the corporal in the general, the clown in God, the son in the father, moralities in chronicle plays, buried women in fortress walls. An intellectual's freedom is his unceasing questioning—the attempt to shake off the role he is incapable of shedding. The ruling intellectual cannot make a revolution against himself so he must make one inside himself. First he should look in the mirror: he is a self-appointed official candidate who shoots at his protector because he wants to become the protector. He flaunts his commitment and plays the hero until the question is put to him in his villa by a TV reporter: does he have faith in humanity? Carefully indicating his painful doubts, he finally nods: yes, he does. Before analyzing the inner structure of institutions, my son thought, he ought to consider the structure of his own poses, and laugh at his utopias, his swagger, his pathos, at the prospective company-president in him, who keeps climbing until he gets to do things he knows less and less about, and is well versed in arguments justifying the unequal sharing of power. Such speculation evoked in my son apostolic frenzy one day, and catatonic chills the next. He filled his mind with the conflicts of his world, but he could not yet forgo the privileges of a clear conscience. If he keeps insisting on these privileges, he will either destroy himself or begin to lie.

I wasn't anxious to explain to him that in a city whose population's greatest wish is to spend one-third of its income on food instead of one-half; where they are hardly ready for new concepts of spatial order, yearning as they are for fifty square meters of living space per family; where among a dozen heads of households only one could call himself, with some exaggeration, an intellectual; where the breakdown of authority, as a rule, goes hand in hand with the looting of department stores and the denunciation of a few detested neighbors before the brand-new authorities— in such a city the radical intellectual learns the paradoxes of serpent wisdom while doing what he knows best, or receives a modest fee for confidential reform schemes that are gradually eaten away by provincial pettiness and the daring affirmation of commonplaces. He may also assume the role of the clown, who is not taken seriously because he is so extremely serious. The clown must understand the sweaty, irritable crowd, so his tricks can have no moral. He is the impossible-to-get-rid-of junkman who offers his shabby but still usable parables to everyone in sight. For him anyone who listens is a good customer, because he encompasses all the others as well as himself.

Instead of abusing the humanists, the clown must abuse himself, especially if those humanists see the essence of humanity in their own inflated self-portraits. He compulsively trains himself in the contradictory tournaments of quick-wittedness and love. He is familiar with the odds of moral integrity, with the rate of exchange of the soul—still, he trusts blindly the first stranger he meets. He doesn't wish to grow from manhood to godhead, for he has learned that if he doesn't restrain the expansionist in him, who knows perfectly how to judge, accuse, excommunicate, he helps to knock out the ground from under his own feet. He can't even survive in heirs, so why can't all his kinfolk look his mortality straight in the eye. His profession demands that he doubt all that is human and that he understand his fellow players even when they are against him. By switching his costumes he absorbs the rules of the game of the stage. We need a king and we need a king-killer; one is as harsh as the other, but a nation enduring its fate needs memorable culture heroes. The clown watches their sumptuous and angry presence more tenderly after he has found out how interchangeable these people are. He has been clowning long enough not to be offended when called a bourgeois, and although he is not the sworn enemy of radical change, he would like to ruminate on the fruits of permanence. He thinks it's sad that he can tolerate himself only when he is intolerable. Now and then he runs into his son, who seeks freedom for—and from—culture. With a frown he passes over the person who introduces himself as a revolutionary and overthrows a system just to become the one who signs his name to laws. (He ought to have done that at the outset without so much fuss.) But even a clown fixes his stare on the person who knows that in the face of human inertia and the frozen strength of institutions, revolution is rolling a stone up a hill; who persists in scrutinizing his fears and his lust for power; who throws light on his well-kept and shallow secrets; who is freer—and therefore more vulnerable—than others simply because the terror accompanying his thirst for freedom surpasses all other terrors; whose utopia consists of a physical-spiritual realm where even the bourgeoisie look upon their works with a hint of irony; who, because he is forever building and tearing down, will be declared a revolutionary after his death, but who would never dare call himself one, for he has no way of knowing just what heights he is scaling. He is the man who moves toward dazzling solar and cellular systems, toward murderous flashes of light in the rickety ship of consciousness. In looking at such destiny-sketches even the clown is overwhelmed, though they remind him very much of the terrified little boy who stands barefoot early in the morning and haltingly describes his nightmares. Only when he sees his mother and father and dips his bun into his hot chocolate does he calm down and declare that he no longer wants to go to kindergarten because there even good things look bad.

Here lies the person for whom I remained in my place. The skin under his eyes and around his mouth is still smooth, but soon my great-grandfather's lunatic features will break through. Among founders and preservers of families there must always be someone who destroys—if nothing else the pitched tent of intelligence, so he can grind his teeth on the thin surface of history. I watch his sleeping face in the hospital room and cover his narrow chest with a light blanket. The hearty clowns are balder, fatter. Insight is born on bloody sheets. The time for revolutions is past. The hospital room is quiet, a nodding patient is chewing a piece of bacon, and is watching my son from the next bed. My thought about the future leads me only to the next heart attack: to arrive there at least means freeing myself from malignant tumors. God, if He still exists, is ironic—the only one who is. My son is not ironic at all, so why not let him clasp an uncertain finger before letting go.

We deny the right of any minority to rule over a majority. Technological revolution must go hand in hand with a revolution in human relations. We first rebelled against feudal privilege, then against private property, finally against bureaucratic authoritarianism. Nobleman, capitalist, intellectual bureaucrat—the actors followed one another's footsteps, but the drama of monopoly is preserved by its weapons, dreams, industries, rituals. The long revolution of anthropology produces a single realization: history offers no solutions; we can only wish for the long revolution of anthropology. The essence of the left is practical criticism of the existing culture, from its technology to its philosophy. The left cannot become obsolete; by switching arguments and spokesmen, it transcends the errors of any one age—it is the thousand-year-old continuity of the spirit. Social revolutions will continue until they make every citizen death-defyingly venturesome. They cannot be content with merely transferring decision-making powers from owners of private property to public officials. The state of monopoly socialism is the temporary manifestation of rule by decree; it can do nothing but watch over the rulers' minor interests. If the revolutionary mind discovers the will of the people in the bureaucratic machinery, with its error it sanctions two of its opponents: inertia and religion. Monopoly is in love with order, but creates a sleepy confusion. It needs theology to put an equal sign between its self-portrait and common experience. The main product of general bureaucracy is the dull-witted, cautious bureaucrat who is irritated by everything that is unlike him. After rejecting his share of the decision-making powers, he simply imprisons himself.

I don't want a city in which pedestrians are chased by warning signs amid ruined or abandoned walls; where nothing is allowed, nothing is possible, nothing is worth the trouble; where ready-made regulations stare at me from shopwindows. I don't want a city where everything stays the same, where suspicion oozes from plaster walls, squares are contaminated by idiotic monotony and a heap of garbage on the corner reminds me of my deformities. I don't want a city where I cower to avoid being snapped at, until I am snapped at for cowering; where greatness is an obtrusion, cowardice is peace, and talk is conspiracy; where I have to like the way things are because they cannot be otherwise; where cunning nobodies search the bunkers of wasted years, and humanity is an irritable substance, a graphic illustration of inattention, the refutation of my hopes, where street-corner lottery-ticket vendors represent transcendence. I don't want a city where turning a crank or looking through a glass tube for eight hours is called work, where a new machine costs more than a dozen men, where I do what I am told and am angriest at the person who asks me why; where, because I overadjust, I am offended by those who adjust less. I don't want a city where periodic tightening and easing of the reins break up monochromatic time, and even ten years is a short time because the price of a three-room house amounts to ten years' pay. I don't want a city where the old hate the young because the latter have undergone too much and the former too little change; where the smartest person in a crowd is always the one who has the greatest store of confidential information, for anyone who is not privy to such information knows practically nothing; where speeches are prayers of thanks, and my bread, my home, my breath are gifts; where definitions are displaced by conspiratorial allusions, reason by zeal, and pointing out logical fallacies is a provocation; where tomorrow, if it doesn't justify today, can be adjourned indefinitely. I don't want a city where the official in charge, though he knows that in half an hour he too will become a client, refuses to deal with the man standing at his desk because everything about him—from his application to his birthmark—is irregular; where showy opposition and moist fear are the bright petals of human character; where it is advisable to wear gray because there is a positive correlation between sartorial grayness and frequency of promotion; where the intelligent pretend to be stupid in order to receive advanced degrees, and incorrect speech is a letter of recommendation. I don't want a city where what I detest is a duty and what I love is immoral, where everyone tries to educate everyone else (all my relatives are prosecutors, judges, executioners); where if I love one human being I cannot love another, and my body, if it desires another body, must feign shame; where I can find joy only in what I own—my son, my dog, my mendacious pictures; where my mother has to perish from her room before my daughter can get married; where the ground plan of apartments teaches us to hate one another; where I tiptoe past the concierge's window, though she knows, all the same, when I get home every day and who comes to see me; where I and my rooms mutually possess each other, though of the two of us my apartment is the more valuable; where the only thing that is mine is what I eat, and I therefore stuff myself, flatter, scrounge, and know that in the next house a similar nonentity has the same fears and the same greedy appetite.

I dream of a city in which action is synonymous with

change, where I have a right to my surroundings, where I don't exist for the city but am wooed by it; where only after consultation with me could decisions be made about me; where people consider the theory of the indivisibility of power a sign of mental deficiency, and observe with amusement the rise and fall of rival factions in the window display of self-government; where I don't have to be satisfied with my meager allotment, and can defend my interests without having to pretend I am helping others; where my friends and I can fire our director as easily as he can fire us; where even the mayor is a temporary civil servant, on leave from his regular job; where I am a reformer because of my ideas, not because I have been appointed; where scarcity does not build a barbed-wire fence around our jealously guarded inequalities, and even a street cleaner's share of the communal property has an effect on the national economy; where I don't have to support the arrogant bunglings of bureaucrats; where no one flaunts his authority and no one is without authority; where I don't have to translate my expertise into jargon, where laws regulate errors, and free citizens can register their free will on electronic voting-machines hooked up in their homes; where there is no capital punishment and my safety is guarded by the quick reflexes of the community; where a department-store manager asks the coat-thief what else he needs, and if he would like to receive a credit card; where the public eye replaces the clout of the penal code, and no one can prosecute me and then say it was all a regrettable error; where contracts curb the excesses of factional struggles, and even schoolchildren ridicule the savage logic that invariably extols the breast-beating victor and spits on the knocked-out loser; where there are no secrets for spies to uncover, and anyone can look at the minutes of official meetings; where at press conferences I express my personal opinion, and I remember that rhetoric is the main subject in an academy for swine;

where the front pages of newspapers contain intellectual revelations, and the community rewards those who are different; where a high school is run differently from a chicken farm, and a teacher teaches by sharing his interests with his students; where everyone can make his thoughts public, but only those who have something to say, and can say it succinctly, have readers; where entire streets are bulletin boards, and everyone can paint the sidewalks and address passers-by; where there is music in public squares and people take pleasure in shaping their environment; where all visible matter is sculpture, and politeness is the exquisite language of the body; where I wouldn't spend hours looking at a name on the door of a house; where I can endure it with serenity if my mate loves someone else, and accept the fact that anyone can love my child; where I would rather loathe myself than flatter others, and would much rather joke in a cemetery than give orders in an academy; where I would try to substitute self-analysis for apology, hypothesis for law, skepticism for faith, discussion for pronouncements, epigrams for editorials, my truths for my opponents', my caricature for self-righteous poses. Instead of observing official holidays I want to join a carnival. I would gladly admit that nothing is mine except my death —and the whole world.

I want a left-wing city, a destructively constructive, diffusely coherent dialogue about the perils of being human; a brazenly contemporary afterworld that is not only thought but also thinking itself; where city planning is a war of liberation fought against dumb, featureless squares, where city dwellers transmit their secret wishes to their possessions, line their bodies with memories, have jurisdiction over their organs, wrest from space new possibilities, and immerse themselves in their culture. The fragile structures of the city are regularly repeated messages from a misshapen void, aimed at our incorporeal mother who in the hall of possibilities plays a cheap little ditty about time and space. Over precarious and crumbling heaps I want unexpected, slender shapes, whose ever-growing possibilities question their own viability—a city that its citizens use to debate and make love in. Through the language of objects they can communicate with the dead, and on their doorknobs shake hands with vanished forebears. I want a city where only what joy guards remains, and where the traffic of innovations is never choked off. I want streets where the eyes of passers-by reveal that something happened to them: they twitched in a spasm of existence and stretched out in lukewarm death.

My father's pitch-beard and polished bald pate emerge for a moment from the back of an armchair. He puffs up his cheeks and gets ready to deliver a short lecture; his burning cigar will mark his points. He puts his hand on my shoulder, but directs my attention to his beard, which is swarming with worms. Before leaving for the construction site early in the morning, he looks back and strokes his beard. I sneak after him: he smells my head, I smell his leather jacket. He mumbles with feeling: there is snow on the flagpole. Bacon glitters on the table. This leather-bound album contains pictures of his houses, all of them completed as planned. I take daily walks in my father's

SEVEN

thoughts. He finishes an apartment house in a matter of weeks; before a strike he screams, but pays. He builds a fort over our heads, and during supper he half listens to my mother's tuneful babble, to him a confirmation of its stability. The great white sheepdog brings back the twig from the river twenty times. In the morning, while the barber is giving him a shave, he looks over his city from the terrace. On most streets there are homes with marble plaques bearing his name, which is also engraved on a brass plate on the aldermen's table in City Hall. He emerges from his bedroom in his red robe, does a few push-ups, and swings his arms; my mother lies in bed and watches him from distant, wavy plains, her knees trembling. Father carves up the turkey with a brass-handled knife. He'll soon be done with his roast and will pull me over. His fat, hairy hand reaches out from his study and pulls in the maid. I see them through the clouded glass of the dining-room door: he shakes her out of her skirt and, grabbing her under her knees, lifts her up to his stomach. The red chest-hair of this man, who is mad about quince jelly and walnut liqueur, is a well-known family trait. On his way home from the council meeting, my father's head is like a brass samovar: he keeps puffing the mayor's name. He revels in slanders—from his back, sated leeches fall off one by one, a firecracker burns the fingers of his raised hand. He draws in his stomach and asks my sister to dance; with three taps on the bottom he pops the cork from the wine bottle. They are again gossiping about me and a woman, he complains. My mother smiles sympathetically. We are sitting in the back of the wagon; father is in the driver's seat. He has just conferred with God in church. We ride under plane trees, a dragonfly lands on his whip, we are light as bubbles. Father grabs me by the collar and shakes me violently. You dared to do this! he screams, and would like to crush me with his feet. He rips off the curtains, and is finally calmed by the church bell. He slumps down next to the piano, his elbow still leaning on the keys. The dusty chords smoke in the reflected light of the snowy garden. Now he is walking in flesh-colored deserts; prickly iron fortresses rise from under the sand.

What is this weight on my chest? he asks as I touch his forehead. First only my fingers perceive the message relayed by cold sweat and slowing pulse: I cannot much longer call this collapsing mass father. But so long as he returns my glance I keep calling his name. I don't want him to die alone, behind the white metal partition of the isolation ward. I don't want them to saw off the dome of his skull or cut open his belly, just so we could have it on paper that no one is to be held responsible for his departure. He dreads hospitals, and wouldn't let go of my mother's hand—the holy family is inviolable. The doctor bites his lips until he finds the vein, mother presses the rubber hose, and five minutes later father's face is flushed with color, his forehead is dry, his feet warm, his consciousness is back. A sandbag was on my chest, he complains. He is drinking tea now and wants to know how long he must stay in bed. God, he has a million things to do—must get a new construction under way, make a report to a committee, patent a new invention. He tries to sit up and knocks over the reading lamp. A little later he motions me to come closer and whispers into my ear: I will die. He watches me with shy curiosity, ashamed, perhaps, of what he said, but I do not protest. He has something else to say before letting me go: You see now what life is all about. It no longer matters to him if I understand. He takes his eyes off me and smiles cautiously, as if he had just been apprised of some extraordinary news. My dearest, mother says. With wide-open eyes she looks at his large face, whose every frown at the dinner table was a natural disaster. She also looks at the blackening row of teeth under the gold bridges, at the shirt-tearing fingers that never again will make her headache go away. She looks into his eyes—a theater of vanished time, whose dismissed director is giving a farewell performance. Then a choked guttural sound that is no longer father's: his tongue seems to roll back into his throat, I can't feel his heartbeat or hear him breathe. Every son is curious about his father's death. The doctor steps in from the other room. I can see from here he is dead, he says, and is somewhat proud he can see from there. Mother protests in a faint voice; we are quiet for a while, and then she says: A moment ago he was still alive. She repeats this a few times, almost imploringly. First she kisses his mouth, then closes his eyelids and folds his arms over his chest. I am amazed she knows how to do these things. Push up his chin, too, says the doctor, and signs a piece of paper that makes the death official. When we are left alone I put my arms around her. She can't cry, only soft moans well up in her, now and then she gives a shudder. We sit down next to father—she at his head, I at his feet. It's three o'clock, there is nothing to do. The first half hour of eternity smoothes out father's face; little by little his lips lighten, and no longer clash with the color of his cheeks. First his arms get cold, then his body; it's cold in the room, too. By next morning his temperature is the same as the room's. We drink tea, I finish off father's wine, mother combs his hair. It's as if he were asleep, mother says. As I pull off his signet ring my hand is as red as Esau's. It is noon when they come for him. I try to cry in the garden, but only a few, faltering sounds come out. Never mind, I am going for the death certificate. Father is still that cold object inside on the moist bed. A few more chores and then next week: nothing. At City Hall I have to wait a while before seeing a rosy-cheeked, smooth-skinned young man who enters father's name in a table-sized book with indelible ink.

◻   ◻   ◻

The funeral bells begin to ring in the cemetery, and the farewell-parody gets under way—the pop-kitsch-carnival of the last rites, the final social event of a biography, the homage our bafflement pays to fact. Dressed in his best suit, father, like a birthday boy, waits for us on the bier. His nose sticks up under the silk shroud; with furtive curiosity, I pull the shroud down to his necktie—his lips are as yellow as his forehead. His neck twisted, he lies uncomfortably under an arch of wax roses, paper leaves, and plastic-and-wire evergreens. Next to his freshly shined shoes, in the cast-iron floor-lamp, a feeble, fly-specked bulb flickers. I walk around the room, and in the corner, under an eight-armed wall-fixture filled with candles, I draw aside a bulging curtain: another corpse is waiting in the wings, and behind it a third. Room must be made for all of them on the bier. In the faint scent of his decomposing flesh, the solitude of his body is as yet unbroken. A hideous, drooling guard stands next to me; he glances at the corpse expertly, like a pastry chef sizing up a cake already topped with strawberries and roasted nuts. Under the greasy peak of his hat, he calmly eats a piece of buttered bread. Minutes later my mother appears, supported on both sides, stumbling toward the final rendezvous with her husband, who has absolutely nothing more to say to her. He hides under the light summer cover, just as he did when she approached his bed, washed and scented under her arm and on her thigh, and, kneeling on him, pulled off the sheet. Then, in the noisy joy of reunion she had searched his mouth, and stuffed it with the pointed nipples of her heavy breasts. But time has done its work on her breasts, too, and this is a summer blanket she wouldn't dare touch, a mouth she would rather not kiss, only the forehead, whose coolness is more congenial to her lips. She does touch the sunken eyelids, and finally pulls the shroud off father's clean-shaven face. As though suddenly struck on the face, she begins to cry.

Because I do not believe that what I see is only a coat left behind; because every moment is plan and decision until I manage to lock things into an unchangeable present; because my consciousness is a continuous effulgence, while father's is the diminishing and finally vanishing light of a turned-off TV screen; because I cannot follow his retreat with my aggressive, inquisitive intellect—though I watched many people die, I cannot leave without a shudder of ignorance this temple of derision, my father's house, the rotting philosopher's stone, the frontier marker of the end of the world, and this canopied bed under whose baldachin of wax roses I will one day lie. Oh, if I only knew a little more about myself than the ox that will soon have its horns tied to the raised sideboard of a specially designed truck and be taken for a last ride; if I only had some tangible means of sizing up the choices still left to me! I must know, if only for an instant, what will become of me without my tormenting questions, while waiting, between two candelabras exuding incense, for my visitors and the enumeration of my achievements. And what became of father, my accidental and brotherly prototype, this soft death-mask, this arching, narrowing, though not totally lifelike copy of his last week's self; this obscured attention, this wrinkle-free finality, this inert inward-turning, this curtained-off projection screen, this invulnerable nonpresence, this torn-up declaration of independence, this invalidation of a long list of regulations, this perfect match with collar and fob chain from which the watch has been removed, this slice of space on whose salver one could place a glass of water as easily as on a tabletop, this de-electrified bundle of wires in the bone basket of the skull, this hollowing in of all surfaces, this purple-bluing of back and buttocks after a temporary *rigor mortis*, this greening stomach lining, this pervasive summer decay, this uninhabited house slated for demolition, this citizen to whom laws no longer apply, this unrepeatable reason for associating two consecutive phone numbers in an address book, this name on a coffin, which hurried pens have scratched from the starting list of every contest, this over-long question that found its answer once and for all, this city of experience that, within minutes, turned into a desert, this giant library that is now outwitted by a worm, this irresponsible typewriter that stopped in midsentence, this emptied exhibition hall, this abandoned fairground, this mist rising over the crown of weeping willows and black pines. If I could learn something about that other side, about father's domain, everything would change here, too; but because even he can't whisper into my ear the one word that would put me at ease, I remain a raging ox, and they might as well turn up the current in the electrified wire of my pen.

Stone-lilies, stone-grapes, stone-angels, glazed-faced Christ fashioned from rock, a stone-athlete sinking on his shield, a nude stone-dancer, tiny castles placed next to candles and flowers, white marble citadels, a bronze head looking down at its grave with green sorrow, a black marble couple in their Sunday finest, complete with watch chain and necktie, sandstone general with epaulets and two stars, red-lipped stone-photographs, laminated permanents and diamond necklaces, gun barrels and shovel handles, joined to form makeshift crosses—memorials to well-cared-for and forgotten dead. Under the row of chestnut trees lie the distinguished citizens of my city; in front are beribboned counts and decorated generals, bank presidents, directors of mines, mayors, privy councilors, prelates, newspaper publishers. The **gil**ding on their man-sized tombstones is long faded. They are followed by more generals, and council presidents, police chiefs, prosecutors, general managers, department heads, academicians, state-prize-winning artists, who lie under freshly gilded, waist-high tombstones. Even the newer titles are beginning to acquire a special flavor. I experience the transcendence of stone flowers and flowery words. Human pathos runs wild under birdhouse-laden oak trees.

All of these people left us an eternal legacy; beyond the grave our love accompanies everyone. The unforgettable dead are rewarded for their labors with tombstones befitting their social position; they are the envy of people residing in the outer reaches of the cemetery. In extolling the dead, the people of my city sing their own praises. The privileged dead, before they came here, fought their battles, and insulted, ostracized, imprisoned, and finally decorated one another, while the masses marched under their heroic statues, from a past that was all bad into a future that was promised to be all good. Then, one by one the leaders retired to the relative safety of grave plots on the main street of the cemetery.

Across the way is the columbarium—the residential area of the cremated. Eight urns can be stacked on top of one another in compartments twenty centimeters wide and forty centimeters deep. In some cases, spouses move into the same compartment: each deceased is therefore allotted an average of one square decimeter of space. As a city planner I feel I ought to approve of this quintessentially economical solution to the problem of space shortage in an industrial society. The one-family home, as well as the private grave, is a thing of the past; parts of this city, populated by the modern, democratic dead, spread vertically. The compartments are cemented in on all four sides by book-sized concrete sheets; a metal knob is attached to each sheet.

A five-digit number, as well as the name of the deceased, is inscribed on each of the boxes, but no social rank, date, or farewell phrase. The hunger for titles and gold-engraved rhetoric is forced to yield to a system of social justice that, within the confines of this necropolis at least, has vanquished inequalities. However, individual efforts are already beginning to undermine the residential equality. An irregular little stone plate is glued on one of the compartment walls: Sweetest mother and wife, rest in peace. The possibilities for decoration are limited: glasses, aluminum cans, preserve jars, tiny vases dangle from string tied to a stone handle; in them visitors have put strawflowers, pussy willow, bunches of dried daisies. I see a bit of grayish ooze in the bottom of a jar; black bugs took over the aluminum can. The more prudent visitors place hardy artificial flowers on the metal knobs and, lately, plastic fruit—bananas, peaches, bunches of grapes. Those with a more baroque taste utilize the space even more cleverly: they fasten small shelves on the enclosing wall, and put tiny tubs and towers on them. The bouquets can be more handsomely arranged on these shelves. With their eyes closed, their collars unbuttoned, people stand in front of these tiny contraptions, which are supposed to evoke the features of the departed loved ones. Here, they think, they can remember them, and murmur a prayer, with greater feeling. Soon this will be no mere residential area but a veritable city—functional, realistic, its formal elements perfectly consistent with its essential purpose. This wall, though containing the urn into which my wife's remains were swept, is enough to make me laugh in death's face.

There is an unweeded spot near the wall of the cremated. Fine plants, planted by a gardener long ago, grow amid uncut grass: Chinese woodbine, sumac, Japanese cornel, Western thuja, Eastern barberry. In the shade of silver lindens and ash trees I see the mostly stoneless graves of those who died in January 1945. Here is a twenty-year-old artillery cadet. The armored car swept away the paving stones of his makeshift barricade, and the machine gunner, seeking protection behind the tower of stones, stabbed him in the side. Moments before, the cadet's bazooka accidentally hit his friend, who was riding in the next tank. A quirk of topography and an inaccurate aim could have saved my classmate. I can see his handsome face as he twirls his drumstick in the school band and tosses his hair back when striking the cymbals triumphantly. Next to him lies an old Jew who was summoned from behind a drainpipe by Nazis checking identity papers and shining flashlights into people's faces one night in a cellar. The old man's documents were clumsy forgeries; he could recite the Lord's Prayer, but Hail Mary he couldn't manage, so he had to lower his pants right there in the cellar; and because the foreskin was conspicuously absent from his wizened penis, they hauled him off to a nearby park, and, on the eve of the Russians' arrival, shot him into a blue-tiled wading pool. Here is a little boy who went out to see his mother in the yard while she was cooking bean soup over her burning dining-room chair. She was about to taste the soup with a wooden spoon when a fighter plane flew over their block, and a stray volley hit the boy in the head. His mother just saw him topple over and fall on the soup, which was now dripping through a hole cut in the pot by a bullet. They all died accidentally: soldiers and deserters, Christians and Jews, armed men and fugitives, the hopeful and the terror-stricken, natives and refugees, informers and informees, Germans and Russians, Europeans and Asians, people who had killed, people who had never killed, people who *were* killed. Large insects crawl between the toppled-over grave markers, rabbits chew sour leaves, a porcupine suns itself on a molehill—life is much too alive here. Some picnickers made a fire on stones piled atop a grave; you can still see the grease spots left by bacon clumsily turned on the spit.

A young butcher built a cozy arbor here. He eats meat all day so he can receive unfulfilled divorcees, who for a modest fee pant on him for an hour, and entwine their not-so-young thighs around his neck. Trailed by a gust of perfume, the pathologically obese wife of a sad, aged library-director presses into the arbor. Her nymphomania requires periodic psychiatric treatment, but now she comes to this boy, who is the only one who can get to her unhappily sensitive organs. As he does, she mutters the licentious poetry of relief, her voice blending with the din of sparrows about to retire for the night.

Leaning on a silver-handled cane, her varicose veins bulging, mother, in her ruffled neckband, used to come here, too, to visit father. She brought a basketful of tools, and even wrapped her toothbrush glass in silver foil. She planted slender little trees around the grave, and had a red bench put in front of it. I can see her digging holes with a shovel and stuffing potted flowers in them. Father's grave stands there like an overdressed rich boy at a village school graduation. An entire Japanese garden covers the grave; tiny blue spruce, golden cypress, prickly rosebushes, holy basil, cactus—she practices scientific gardening, making sure the grave is in bloom every season of the year. A multi-story castle with many tiny wings; in one of them a toy soldier sounds the trumpets of redemption each morning above father's head. His grave is a memorial to clear conscience—it is worth it to lie in it. My mother came here every day for twenty-five years. She put her white gloves on the castle and set about watering and housecleaning. I loved to see her busying about the grave. She didn't submit to decay, her routines triumphed over all chaos. No one minded when a young couple kissed; and when an old man upbraided them—There is to be no kissing here, this place belongs to God and the dead—and made ready to summon the caretaker, my mother raised her stick. Stupid old man, she said, God loves those who love each other, because God is—and here she faltered—is no stickler for rules.

Sunlit bells ring; the pearly dome of lunch's fragrance

hangs over man and dog waiting on the kitchen threshold. Somebody's son toddles around a playpen, a baby stork flutters about a chimney. On the bridge a huddled group of convicts pass. A gravedigger in shirt sleeves pits plums for jam on a bench in front of his house. God watches man, man watches the fox, the fox watches the owl, the owl watches the shrew, the shrew watches the worm—tell, O stars, whom does the worm watch, the worm that crawled into my brain weeks after the funeral? If someone said that a kind of transcendence resides in the worm's brain I would believe him—let it brood over the finitude of its existence while it devours me. If the same eye watches both of us, its total presence amounts to infinite abandonment. It murders and crumbles in my hand; wherever I reach, I touch it. It is either everywhere or nowhere; either way we can't communicate. But if it exists in one place and not in another, only my religious instructor could enlighten me as to its whereabouts; and if I ask too many questions, he will report me to the principal. There must be a place in the universe where all the animals of creation gather and ridicule one another. Attendance is not yet perfect; we can go on assuming airs for a while longer, but if everyone were to find this place, we could liquidate the entire world.

We must put an end to this growing, throbbing pain, this self-imprisonment in the projection room of sentimental losses. If the chain of present moments loses its link with the reveries of the future, if my life is but a usurpation of names and objects, a desperate clinging, after the final, nonappealable judgment and the rejection of my last clemency plea, to the window bars of my dungeon; when objects turn away from me or fence me in; when, having performed my seemingly real tasks, I believe I can go beyond plain perception—then I come here, I must come here. Because the cemetery talks of nothing but the insane passion for survival. It tells us that we have nothing to do with death, that there is no death, only this carnival, this travesty, this idiotic museum of anxious contortions, this beastly hunger, this sophomoric wit, this choreography of vanities. If others tolerate me in no man's land, road, city; if I can buy food with my money and get money for my time; if the warm smell of wild flowers can penetrate my lungs; if by connecting rods or figures I can still contribute to my culture, then I will linger a little longer among my fellow citizens and look in their faces without hunger or hate.

My back takes on the ship's cumbrous sway. Pressed between the sky-blue sea and the sea-blue sky, I lie on a disk of light. Below me the ship's propeller cuts wrinkly, dark chambers in the glassy surface. A baptismal voyage: the wind blows salt-water spray on my lips. I try to resist my god-faced demons: in a cool summer shirt life is one delicious stretch, the polished bench I am sitting on whisks me to a utopia. Blue-gold foam wipes from my face the double-twist knots of tax collectors. I look at my tooth marks on the flesh of a banana, at the shrubbery lining the bay; I pretend to have free time on my hands, and begin to resemble a human being. On this island of chapels and lacy clouds, I see the grooves left by icequakes on mountain

EIGHT

slopes: marauding time has crumbled their treeless tops. As from a disaster I avert my glance from snow-white limestone peaks—I am a builder, it seems, to the marrow of my bones. Dazzled by a momentary flash of freedom, and feeling somewhat ill, I am bringing my aging and increasingly suspicious life to a city that I hardly know. I put all my chips on a red adventure, but the wheel stopped on a black number. The outcome of the game was determined by degrees of longitude and latitude on the map. I wanted to plan a city, but it had plans for me, creating a dream from which I will one day awaken. I turned out all my pockets, covered my dead with marble, paid all my debts. Sentimental journeys always take their toll.

I loll between canvas lounge-chairs billowing in the wind, on a deck fading into the future. A scene from the postindustrial vision of expanding free time: liquescent bodies lying all around, paper cones falling off nose ridges, unfolding thighs, postnatal skin with netlike patterns surrendering to sunlight, brown scars of old operations tanning in strips. Dry, veiny, sunburned legs bend and stretch out; the body itself makes its peace with the world. We take away nothing from and give nothing to one another. In the tranquil freedom of the seas, the self-centered, separated bodies loosen up; only their orifices, assaulted by the heat waves of sensual excitement, are busy working, as waiters whirl about with trays, offering cold chicken, ice cream, orange juice.

Upstairs, on the first-class deck, a young man steps into the viewfinder of a camera held by a kneeling photographer. He sits on the rail and lets everyone admire him; his body exudes joy, brutal lust—a shield I hold up for a minute between my opened fingers and old age. I forget the cooled-off room where two rowdy lovers become two scrubbed books of etiquette. I forget the mutual recriminations of two people who are unable either to violate or to observe the rules in peace. I am happy about the mortality of my lust; I close my eyes: animals with heads for legs surround me on the stone floor of an empty room.

White-bellied, gray-backed seagulls whir overhead, the sun shines through their downy wing-quills; after eighteen strokes comes a long, hovering glide—they are sailing on the wind's hammocks. Their gleaming, black-hooded heads and crooked beaks turn left and right, surveying the ship and the sea lane behind it. Spies, detectives of the sky, they drop on the water in mid-flight to catch fish churned up by the propeller. They are angels of doubt fluttering over my brow, Knights of the Temple guarding the skies, soaring crosses above passionate and detestable flesh. Air itself designed their firm tail-feathers, the arch of their bones, their bulletlike heads. They are indifferent jewels on a perfect sky, and their flight is a flawless festival and hunt. Quick, screeching fight for a head, a tail: they want neither to solidify nor to change things. They fly over absences and over the repulsive alliance of virtue and vice. They don't differentiate between their nourishment and themselves, and therefore do not pay for that extra knowledge with the incurable disease of the ego. Mine are the imaginary wings of inquiry and judgment—theirs are time's pathos-free sentences, and the wide open space of the present stretched out above nourishing waters and cities. In the universal marketplace who shopped better? They are repeated in their progeny and in the recurrent events of eternity, and have no need for community. They team up indiscriminately, soar with nonexistent self-awareness, pilot their own wind-defying bodies. They are my masters, these seagulls.

In the first-class swimming pool, in secluded bays, in the water holes of memory, in the aquamarine cisterns of summer, bodies recognize their basic element. Legs, accustomed to forced marches in culture deserts, recall an ancient rule of traffic: all roads are main roads. The daydreams of an amphibious age, a round world of the senses, the interchangeability of water, earth, air—an illuminated landscape under the crescent of consciousness. The planner's tricks can't be wedged into the crevices of history, whose desire to attain eternal peace produces never-ending wars. Being here is enough of an accomplishment; our wretched consciousness need not impose itself on the world, it need not pull itself out of warm ooze to chase even more gruesome utopias. Under a great brass ceiling, in a viscous fluid, bodies copulate, and learn the choreography of movement and suspension. They are spy satellites in the salty night, shields on the layers of tender oblivion—the fingers of a drunken pianist who doesn't know what he is fingering on his somewhat stupid, somewhat beautiful, sated blonde piano.

Let's salute; there are war games on this beach. Chalk-white typists step out of the dressing room with aggressive self-doubts. How they would like to circle at least the first day of their vacation with red ink in their pocket calendars. Generously applying oil on their bodies, they get dressed for a daylong operation, letting the sun's scalpel pierce through them. Protruding crosses on blankets of expectation, the slow procession of a hand in love with a thigh, desert wrinkles on shaved underarms, brownish discoloration on legs raised for intercourse, surrenders, admissions: where is the mechanic who will fix up these bodies? On retinas, Saint George gallops on an unbridled gelding, his hair spread out on his purple robe; lances strike dragons; a knight reviews a field of flesh, women's wombs burn. Soft-bodied families slide out of their moist shells, heads of households, still on this side of retirement parties and silver anniversaries, turn away from their wives, who guard their lower parts with the same torturous pride with which an invalid shields his artificial limbs. Smells emanate from chapped orifices, lovers eat from each other's mouths—if they were to rise from a common grave they would still recognize each other, and loll on a celestial beach. The loudspeaker is ready to drop a stern request into the fishbowl of good humor, a single body is entitled to two square meters of space, streets form even here, members of the naked society prefer not to see their neighbors. Stripped of their uniform of ostentation, they all reveal the ravages of time—deformations, cave-ins, needless accumulations or erosions—cozily misshapen spouses in sunlight's display window. Many bodies have become orphaned objects; the semidarkness of their embraces had given way to the blinding light of interrogating rooms, until indifference replaced hostility, and they changed back into windows on the wall of objectivity. Guilt appears on the concrete walkway in the shape of a muscular, well-proportioned brown body. This is how a body should be composed; this is the way to retain our hold on stomach, thigh, shoulder. It is he the underdogs of nudity vie for; they want to possess this slender structure, explore it and live in it. A slight wind chases butterflies above penitent bodies; the carpet of flesh laughs —this may be the last day of peace; tomorrow the last judgment, or autumn's fighter-bombers, might hover over the sundecks.

As my body awakens slowly, cell by cell, in the dark pool, I peer anxiously at my fellow bathers: which livid spot on their rolled-up bodies are they trying to soak off in the iodized water; between the dividing ropes of what fears are they panting so furiously; what rebellion in their bodies are these stubborn swimmers suppressing? After having swum their laps, completed the self-prescribed breathing exercises, stood on their heads, and torn themselves away from the steamy, soapy, sulphurous shower, they, too, will probably ask themselves: how would their bodies like to appear in the dim light of a night-table lamp when, recovered from a day of proper standing, sitting, bowing, they embrace another body; when someone grasps these firm back muscles, these buttocks, this rare genital; when someone is entwined by these lean thighs? And how would those like to be seen who fall asleep with the radio playing and the lights burning; who are happy when gentle finger-strokes turn their hungry fantasies into a hot substance. However they appear, they are swimming against the current of time. I study, like an anatomical chart, my waking body, and am disarmed by its exertion. My own body gives me the key to unlock others; and I am almost moved by the nakedness of sunbathers lying on the deck this fading summer day.

I myself could ask this body: what was it after? It rushed me when I tried to sleep, detained me when I wanted to go, turned my own judgments against me, wrecked my plans, involved me in deceit and shame, locked me up with the monotonous refutations of my well-being. It lay down on any bed, rubbed against any body, took samples from vast quantities of eager flesh, founded new territories of carnal pleasure, and even redundant thighs and bellies didn't deter it from fruitless new experiments. In a cruel test of faith, it donned vestments and received and offered communion until exposed by its obscene prayer. What god did it serve? Who imposed on it such a regimen of exercises? It had to bury itself in the hollow of another neck, hold another tongue between its teeth, leave its finger marks on a back, sharpen nipples, lick thighs. What made it break down safety locks, gallop across state borders, and cut through the electrified fence of morality? After light summer love-making came a heavy-cloaked blackout, when knives were so handy, when an astonished butcher gave one last stab, when primordial inequalities were restored, when two nailed-down coffins futilely knocked against each other. Strangulations, karate chops—formidable messages from the battleground of the body. Drying skin in the cupboard of memory—why did this hand want to wipe off the horizon? The one without whom I couldn't sleep, whose thigh I had to touch in trains and parks, who had more fragrance behind her ear than a flower stall, whom I lifted high many a time and who shrieked with joy, whose every flaw I blindly forgave—why did I torment her while she was alive?

A rusty buoy floats in the middle of the blue-gold bay, amid a cluster of fruit barges. A funnel of seagulls hovers over the buoy. Orange trees, heavy with fruit, line the waterfront. Farther back is an amusement park with fairy-tale cottages and tomato-red sunshades. On the emblem of an ammunition tower and on a brass clock's dial plate, a silver whale carries the city across the waves of centuries. This is the kind of city I tried to draw during Christmas vacation, after a sleigh ride, while apples baked in the tile stove and my lead soldiers took cover under the piano. A wrist-thick rope twists on the mooring posts of the harbor; tourist faces break up the unity of the stone wall that stretches between two waterfront inns. Sleepy octopus faces emerge from coral hollows; as soon as the ship departs they sink back on their pillows. Water boils up between two cliffs; seahorses swirl before the inexorable hour of fertilization. A motorboat speeds toward a slowing ship: a skinny boy stands in its prow, and next to him a tousled girl who smiles at him unabashedly. After reaching shore she will fall on his heavy thigh on slimy steps. In the rippling water crabs crawl out from under mossy stones. Widows from the north, with fig leaves pressed to their noses, soak up the sun in wide-framed barges. Thick-testicled teenagers ride their bicycles along the shore. A sailboat approaches, kicking up a cloud of water-dust; in its bow a girl guts a fish. Holding a dagger in her bloody right hand and the clean fish in her left, she waves—a tableau of triumph. The ship's horn is sounded, the drawbridge is about to be lifted. I step ashore; whatever I need will come to pass.

I put both my hands on your skull; your waist is as slender as my rosewood pipe; salt and light have washed away your grief. I am insanely happy to see you: we exist and others don't. On this entire island you are the wildest dancer—we shall buy adhesive tape for your ankles; your jeweler landlady may rent me a room, too, on the main square. I wasn't being good, only defenseless, when, having climbed over the wall of the reform school, you stepped into my palm. Tormented, water-spouting gargoyles: symbols of medieval love and jealousy; dried crab apples on grave-white paving stones; starfish in nets stretched between stakes; strawberries and promenade concerts in front of the spa that is a relic of the Austro-Hungarian monarchy. We digest our dead; show me the way. Elbow-jointed streets ascend in tiers toward the vaulted cathedral, their shady corners echo every word and step. Boarded-up archways, coats of arms with harpoons between stone eagles, cypress, ivy, and rotten bark where halls used to be. Light plays its maternal games on the engraved names of families. Under a broken column an old woman with a ravaged face watches a drying, empty nest on top of a chimney. We turn into such simple things—let me buy you something, a brass-buckled belt, a choker, a piece of Turkish delight.

In the school garden I stand over Celtic horse skulls, axes, jewelry, and crumple the invitation to your midsummer-night show. You suddenly turn up and make it easy to remember you. Your body covered from head to toe with clippings from magazines: a male beauty contest on your breast, an execution on your rump, a royal couple on your thigh. You dashed up and down frantically, sounding like a ram's horn; during a mad-dog dance you seemed ready to scatter your limbs on the dinner tables. You were a living pickax, a hand grenade ready to be thrown, and then a fugitive with a marked face, pursued by predatory instinct across locks, bars, walls. The director watched your anti-censorship production and got hysterical; with a whistle blow she put an end to it. I knew I would help you; the professional fugitive always finds a toilet window to drive his fist through, and another madman to tumble into a clothes basket with. A week later I fell out of you, half dead, and watched you stretch out your feet on the main square—an extension, I thought, of the fountain's water spout. Your manner of love-making was neither too regular nor stifling. Leaning your head on my shoulder, you lived through the flourishing counterhistory of this baroque square.

From the church square, you can see the sea through eight streets. On the lower end of the bay, ships are anchored. From their stone-framed windows, a butter-colored tourist girl hangs up a red bra and panties on a clothesline strung out between two palm trees—her under-arm hair glitters in the sun. A pair of eyes from under a squashed straw hat watches her secretly. From a bend in the road I can see a sailboat gliding toward the shore in a gentle angle. In front of her street-level apartment, a woman squats before a fire, roasting a peppery leg of pork on an iron grill. Time to write picture postcards. The stone is warm; near the lion-adorned entrance the museum guard lays his head on his table and sleeps. Nuns return from market, carrying bunches of bananas on a stick. We drink red wine and absorb the silence; you rest your feet on the crossbar of the table. From my select stock of images I pick out ones you know, too; I kick in the store's shutter, you chew your fist, and crouch and hiss behind the cracked, corrugated iron sheet, on the oily floor of the stuffy room.

You hold on to the bars of your bed with webbed fingers and press my mouth on your lap as I clasp your sun-polished waist. A sphinxlike smile on a faded blue pillow; you press my ankles, your stomach muscles are taut ropes—what are those lewd eyeballs after? You have immense arms and thighs; in the strait jacket of rapture I gasp like a fish. I laugh at the sweetness of your gifts; you shine under the shower, and put your hand on my head so I will not bang it on the half-closed shutter. Now I only see the veins under your ankles, can only feel you across the iron door, which I will keep on kicking even if you go on hissing and chewing your fist. In the jeweler landlady's shopwindow, old rings lifted from shipwrecks repose next to scorpion necklaces carved from tortoise shells. The city's angel-faced idiot carries a chessboard under his arm and asks you to play with him. In a silk dress cut low enough to expose her belly, the landlady sways before us on the spiral staircase. Under her eyes she is fifty years old; around her hips, twenty-five. A poor imitation of her own self, she spies on her guests through a fake Renaissance mirror, and at dawn walks arm in arm on the deserted square with the demented chess champion. We are still on the stairs when we decide to ask for just one room. You wash my shirt; I stretch out on the double bed. Why do I laugh at every word you say, and at your taking offense as well? I hold on to you in order to endure myself: it's as good to wake up with you as it is to fall asleep. The landlady bangs her coffeepots, you take in my dry shirt from the window—it can't be that hard to get married. But even now, you know as well as I that we will make life ridiculously miserable for each other.

Don't look at anyone on the street; call the beautiful ugly, the young stupid. Say that you love my wrinkles, and that you feel safe in my arms. Never let my head turn to rock when I see you clutching a coat on the other side of the street. I would like to be free of the tenderness of the flesh, free to watch you toss on a strange pillow and scratch unreadable notes on backs younger than mine. I would like to watch good-naturedly a free-style wrestling match, in which limbs thrust out toward freedom. I look at your terrifying topography; why do you offer your throat to be strangled? I wish I had no death wishes. Carnivorous, vain, bored bodies, casualties on the battleground of expansion: they want each other whole and give themselves in part. Plaintiffs and defendants in a no-fault civil suit, they deserve more, but can only get what they give. They are the noisy poor who sever their ties with the world and cultivate a single body, but even so they can't maintain their balance. They shoot moral norms at one another, draw demarcation lines, and fall in a dead faint on thresholds just to obstruct another's path. The lament of leveling-off sexuality; the tiresome superstructures of revenge; wasted years gone forever. I am willing to forgo freedom if I can be sure you are not free, either. Flatter me, tell me tales, caress me, feed me, warm me, clean me; I long to be in a stable, not under the stars; I am afraid of the night. Our instruments of torture fill the stage; we want to be one with everything, while being apart from everything, and end up as two human-looking monkeys, mumbling after God. Perhaps one day, in the ecstasy of suicide, I will finally understand you, and realize that thought is a murderer, and I am cattle and slaughterer rolled into one.

But for the present we stroll between sunshades and olive trees and luscious tomatoes. You smell the iced cases of flatfish, and with vendors guffawing under their bristly beards you haggle over the price of a goblet and curly-nosed slippers. We stick toothpicks in tiny fish fried in oil, and you laugh because I snip off their heads and tails. Meatballs stuffed in grape leaves and onionskin are fast disappearing from copper-topped tables. After drinking the local red wine you address everyone informally, in your native tongue, and are surprised to see the fat pastry-chef in a red fez embracing his fat helper. I watch a black-haired girl—a gliding sailboat with her outspread double cloak of waist-length hair and ankle-length skirt. In a café in the old port, which, amazingly, accommodated galleys laden with Orien-tal rugs, you are asked to waltz to the schmaltzy music of an old-fashioned band. You laugh at the propositions of a Greek seaman, who introduces himself as the captain of a large passenger liner, though I saw him on a ferryboat in the morning. With the passion of adventurers we explore the tiniest alleys of good mood; you look for a room for rent in every house, just to see inside; you touch walls that are insensitive to the passage of time; you watch children around the cathedral rolling balls made out of fired clay just as they did five hundred years ago, when in this slice of the city there already stood the proud institutions of free citizens—a university and a theater. You admire every-thing; a terrorist of joy, you walk around the ramparts, in front of lodgings in which barrel-chested men eat their din-ner, oblivious of the noisy children and cats around them. We roam the rocky mountainside and zoom on a cable car over a monastery, where monks in white hoods read in the bright sunshine. You are dazzled by the dense sea, and dis-cover a bay where for days you hoard stones for a monu-ment. In the evening you light a torch on top of it and welcome a tiny warship. You bask in the sunlight of sympa-thetic glances, and decide to analyze the furrows on people's faces, and even the tavern itself, where strangers join our table unobtrusively and begin conversing without a trace of obsequiousness. Everyone talks politics, and the brawny men, many of whom lost an arm in the war, don't change the subject even when a policeman enters and orders beets and chilled white wine. On a bed that fills our entire room, you stroke the bleached down on your burnt, dry belly. Slinging your legs over my shoulder, you try to convince me that the amount of personal freedom people enjoy can be read on their faces: they can only be nice to one another when they don't have to be afraid. With two minds and four feet I touch the framed scenes of our summer pleasures. I touch the scaly back of a palm tree; I suck on a snail called marine flower. Lamb cooked in wine sauce, olives stuffed with almonds are served along with an immense red lobster, a tender, tasty sculpture that covers the entire table. We crack its claws with our hands. A steel-gray feather flutters on the shell-shaped square; a happy fireman's band passes through. A local holiday, perhaps? No, a holiday of memory.

A torn dream and smoke from burning hemp lift me to an earthquake-stricken city, on whose ruins improbability has pitched its tent. I inspect an overturned telephone booth; a broken-nosed stone lion lies in it, its back still wet from the falling stream of a water fountain. I avoid a well-dressed, limping man as he spreads a blanket over a naked woman who, lifting her legs high amid the broken glass of a chandelier shop, is trying to flee the collapsing wall, or perhaps her husband. I step over the cracked ceiling of the underground urinal; a twisted traffic-light keeps issuing blind warnings. I hear a cry for help: three stories up, an old man stands in a bathtub, with a towel wrapped around his middle. At the edge of the tub a scrawny hen waddles, and

NINE

stares in terror at the gaping hole between the bidet and the sink. The windows of vending machines have flown open; raspberry soda is foaming out of the metal spout, and is dripping on the bronze head of a toppled statesman. On top of a rubble heap a swollen-faced man is crying in a four-poster, and, kneeling on crumbled walls, is shouting a woman's name. Moans rise from the ground. I step into sooty whipped cream and ruined sugar castles; a snow-white rat nibbles on a marzipan fortress. Travel posters soak in the street; fish from a neighboring restaurant's tank wriggle on these golden promissory notes; a rat-hunting cat watches their frantic leaps in disgust. A little girl chases away the flies from her dead brother's lips with her mother's gloves; she would like to straighten out his arm, button his shirt, and she keeps repeating his name—her chores keep her busy.

A girl in a nightgown is wrestling with a tailor's dummy; she would love to undress it. Behind her stands her varicose-veined mother in a pair of men's shoes, telling her angrily that she will go to jail. High above, on the last step of a collapsing staircase, stands a happy couple; the man sings, the woman gestures: she would like to gather the faithful around her. There is no water; fire extinguishers stopped working. Silver-helmeted firemen are condemned to watch burning buildings from the turrets of their fire trucks—they can't even rescue a cat. Laboratory dogs have broken loose from the hospital; with electric wires sticking out of their skulls, and drainage tubes hanging out of their kidneys, they run around in circles; one lies on its side, spreads it feet, and foams at the mouth; another licks a foot sticking out of the rubble. A plaster heap stirs; a head, a trunk emerge. The man is halfway out, but he is ready to give up: I can't feel my legs, he cries. A woman runs up to him, and they embrace. Two ghosts alight from an ambulance; they hold out bandaged hands—their heads are bloody baskets of plaster. Plaster dwarfs, plaster dragons are strewn on the pavement; neon glasses, neon cakes remind us of peacetime appetites. We crunch yesterday's obsessions under our feet—our meager world dismissed us. We were one with our rooms and furniture; we papered our walls with our biographies, and passed an imaginary review stand every day. Now all is gone. We linger in front of our collapsing homes and, when we get tired of waiting, go wherever our feet will take us, carrying our light baggage, and deluding ourselves for a few days that there is yet a new beginning in store for us.

Figures rolled up in patchwork rugs move along the speedwalks of fear toward the demolished lobby of the railroad station: dead mouths, a closed gate; the express trains are stuck. It is said that during the last ten seconds, from which collective forgetfulness would have obliterated the image of an old railroad clerk who disregarded the hoarse directions of dusty loudspeakers and never again asked for the used tickets but went on hating the passengers, remained in his place near the exit, protected himself from the draft, and in the final moments stood up, gripped the palm tree that had bent over him for years, looked at the arriving and departing trains, and made the sign of the cross; in those last ten seconds, which conserved, in slow motion, so many unforgettable, ritualistic trivia (in the eleventh second the railroad station split in two and dropped its ceiling on the glass-walled structure; at the same instant the remote-control switches went berserk: the semaphors turned green, brake linings burst, the entire rolling stock began to move; but this was before the crashing masses of glass and metal destroyed both men and animals; before the sudden, post-cataclysm silence was broken by the desperate whine of an old steam engine, and by bleeding turtledoves whirling under the cracked roof-beams); in those last ten seconds, they say, a pregnant woman rushed after her son, a girl in a money-changing booth stooped under a table to pick up a bill, a soldier on leave dragged a barmaid behind piles of cases into a storage room, and these perfectly indifferent moves were suddenly filled with the enigmatic weight of providence, because through them each of these people was spared. In the background, the granary with its mangled façade and ravaged stock; a flickering gas torch—like a commemorative candle—between sooty flowerbeds and crunching hops. The arena of panic sprawls out before me: beneath the wings of parched cranes a throng of refugees, their hair white from lime. The city burns their feet, this soil can't be trusted; here one day can't vouch for the next. So long as they see its walls they do not turn back. We must leave a place where dreams turn into death, where we wake up one morning on a pile of dust, incomprehensibly remote from our naked, screaming wives.

A column of tanks reaches the bridge, sergeants appear on the turrets of armored cars, on assault guns and fuel tanks—on all horizontal armored surfaces. They squeeze their helmeted heads through the crevices of their steel chambers, and clamber on bulldozers that will smooth out the wrinkles of the earth as though it were a blanket. With walkie-talkies in hand, they keep shouting names of birds and flowers. They come pouring out of dusty barracks yards, camouflaged bases, forest camps; they open up their secret warehouses, push aside jittery civilians, and take over. On the floating mines of their forgetfulness, eye-pleasing field-tables, classrooms adorned with the wrinkle-free portraits of heroes and martyrs, are fast fading; in the excitement of the moment, treasury walls crumble. After so many dry runs, hypothetical enemies, and imagined strikes, the men now have to prove themselves. It's true, of course, that the war itself took place without them, in two minutes, and was as successful as an old-fashioned siege lasting several weeks. But the population is peaceful and can be disciplined. No bearded snipers crouch behind charred roof beams; no one will have to search for aluminum disks in his dead comrades' fatigues—they don't have to kill, only rescue. The season of falling stars is at hand.

The somber act of identifying bodies in the slowly settling dust; no light penetrates the field of rubble. I count the finger marks of heavy blows on the city's mutilated body: its gentle undulations are hardly recognizable at this moment. I survey the inventions of monotonous destruction and senseless simplification: tilted walls, denuded chimneys, colliding columns, towers split in half, domes torn to shreds, statues shot off their pillars, overturned streetcars resembling dead insects, balconies sloping like slides, eviscerated pipes protruding out of walls, iron poles sticking out of concrete like obscenely gesturing fingers, buildings yanked out of their foundations, clumsily disassembled, fused with foreign parts, reduced to their basic elements. Regular outlines replaced by the ragged contours of destruction; the pathetic dimensions of a shrunken geometry. Our vertical challenges of space were reclaimed with a vengeance by gravity, an impudent moment tore to pieces what had cohered for centuries; a half-wit judge severed the legal bond between finely finished objects; an idiotic Peeping Tom broke through the walls of our nakedness; a ruthless opportunist, a machine-wrecking bungler, a disheveled dreamer, finally dislodged the support beams, destroyed the labyrinth of paradoxes, wiped the obstructions of pretense off the face of the earth. Now we stumble on craven matter, outline the unscathed constructs of our paranoias on the permissive soil, reproduce our image in space, and build a new city that will not be responsible for the old. In some ways nicer, this new city is also bound to be more complicated, more difficult to regulate, more uncomfortable than its predecessor. But first we must clear away from under the rubble the prerequisite of a new start: our dead.

If the slogans of supplication were more than mere linguistic exercise, I would wish the peace of a steady light for my son, who probably lies buried here. I can't yet equate him with the dead. They lie in a neat row on the main walk of the cemetery, leaning their heads on old graves destined to be exhumed. Two photographers take pictures of faces from all angles, and of bodies that are either naked or wrapped in rags. For a moment the flash of the cameras fuses with the limy whiteness of their faces. Avoiding the glass-and-earth-encrusted wounds, a uniformed guard's indecently warm hand rolls over the citizens and guests of my city, who wear name tags on their ankles and are immortalized by flash guns for the benefit of latter-day inquirers. I walk up and down in front of glum, paint-smeared statues that are not embraced by screaming relatives. Each familiar lock of hair, toe, chest—until it is made unfamiliar by other appurtenances—makes me turn pale. I know I won't find him among the disinfected objects on display. He disappeared from my city for good under a vault of dust and lamentation. I study his photographs and leaf through his notes. I turn down the hurricane lamp and, from behind my darkened window, keep watching the gutted building on the other side—his thin body and elusive face may yet emerge from the shadows.

I preserve yesterday's trifles, the insignificant liturgy of an autumn Thursday. The buildings stood firm, and wore the languid marks of time. The yelping, evil-sensing dogs had not yet decided to move; the globe-supporting whale with its load of unsuspecting riders was not squirming yet; the cannons of the deep were not yet shooting up waves of tremors; red balls of fire—dirigibles of panic—were not yet scorching lightning's taut ropes; the earth hadn't split; craters hadn't formed; hot water and mud hadn't gushed forth; the grizzled tar on the streets hadn't cracked yet; railroad tracks had not got entangled, and columns of dust —monuments to a stern fate—had not risen in the air to make the entire city one immense chimney. The city was still resting in the palm of peace. The hands of clocks trekked predictably from commonplace to commonplace, until half past six, when all the electric clocks stopped.

In an age of routines, new events are at once holidays and disasters. Let the revolution come, let hurrahs multiply, let things go awry; let's feel strange thighs on the floors of cattle carts, let's drink from the same cup, share a cigarette, rest against one another's shoulders and exchange childhoods. And then let's cast off our circumstances and our own crippled, tormented selves, and wait for a time when the world finally gets tired of its impudence, when rivers return to their beds, and shock becomes a member of the family; when we once again feel the pull of familiar loneliness, and our predictable, worn-out choices regain their rightful place. Whether we rule, or fate does, shock is always followed by cliché, and the golden age of routines is inevitably restored.

Go to the cellar bar, but try not to recall its darker past; don't presume with animistic pride that its walls can remember anything—it is only your deluded mind projecting its nightmares on them. The multipurpose underground chamber, in which we now put our arms around each other's waists, is one of the subconscious recesses of this city. In it the destruction of human bodies was part of a day's work, so think twice before remembering. Here a piece of bread hidden in a pocket got soaked with blood—if you take a good look at the wall, you notice that even repeated paint jobs, or the profile of lovers scrutinizing each other, cannot shield your field of vision from crystallized clots. There were tiny standup cells by the wall; after a two-week confinement in them, prisoners no longer had feet—traitorous trunks leaned on pillars of pain. Eyes were no longer organs of vision but firebrands. Here the soul was forever trying to escape the body, which had to endure pains infinitely multiplying the mundane sufferings of kidney stones and neuralgia. The worst was finding out that they can hit you and you can't hit back; grown men have the right to handle, press, adjust other grown men on the workbench of torture, and create masterpieces of pain. A dentist exemplified human resourcefulness when he packed salt on exposed nerves in a hollowed molar. Men were hanged by their ankles on hooks dangling from the ceiling to make their kidneys and thighs more accessible. Six-foot idiots crushed the testicles of undesirables in their fists. The stakes here were always simple: reveal the name of another man, of a place, or simply say yes. Remember: decent craftsmen built torture chambers for modest wages and promised secrecy, knowing all along that it was their fellow citizens who would be put on the rack. No verdict or explanation can mitigate this disgraceful episode in the city's history. Each employee here could have avoided injuring those sacks of pain, who only an hour ago were called out of offices, pulled down from attics, lifted from underground cells, and brought here blindfolded. All the people who worked here, at the cost of minor unpleasantness, could have refused the job. But they began to relish the idea of being able to do anything with a man who was somebody outside and nobody in here. Pupils could sit their teachers on an electric chair and slowly turn up the current. The more inquisitive among them conducted experiments: at what point do tendons tear, how resistant are stomach muscles, what do cracking teeth sound like when boot heels invade a mouth? What does it take to make a leading citizen of the town, after whom a street would be named if it were not for this interlude, crawl on his knees and devour his own excrement? Curious people recognized the dull freedom of murder, and were almost moved by the stubbornness with which consciousness clung to a body peeled with a razor. It was there they learned the ecstasy of contempt; whoever became their prey complied with their weirdest whim. After having had one eye gouged out, most prisoners begged them to spare the remaining one.

There were a few people who wouldn't say a word even after their organs were permanently damaged. Incredibly, there were some who even rose to challenge their jailers. It was incomprehensible that in human matter that wallowed in blood and excrement, in flesh scorched by torches, gnawed by acid, cut up by knives, there should appear signs of resistance. Battered near-corpses, which in their tormentors' minds had already merged with all other people, their mothers, their fathers, chose to become complete corpses, and clung to a kind of insanity that transcended them and each moment of their existence. A heap of flesh had a distant, imaginary, irrepressible, and radiant double, an abstract counterpart in the depth of its besieged consciousness, which was more powerful than the agonies of the moment. The jailers began to fear this distant figure, though it also enabled them, during the hours of negative rapture, to keep working on the collapsing masses before them. They already had the names they were looking for, but they wanted him to say them. They could not be sure until he was unsure. They tried to free themselves daily of the shudder that seized their iron fist before a still-unmutilated body and encircled it with fear's protective ring; even so, terror in them spread like cancer, and the first blow always made them scream. Swollen with fear, they dragged their pasty bodies in the shadow of tall buildings. And they continued torturing their prisoners even after they had con-

fessed everything. Torture, like resistance, exists for itself—
they are two clashing desires groping their way toward
death.

Adventurers on the edge of existence, they changed
places at times. During the endless hours spent together
under the glaring light of these rooms, an unhappy physical
intimacy developed between aggressor and victim. The two
men, one of whom was pressing the other's hand with the
leg of his chair, sensed each other in their bones. They
realized that a body could be violated even in blessed
silence. These walls also saw a hangman kneel before his
victim and implore him to look back at him just once, and
with a burning shriek acknowledge his existence. He not
only waited for the moment when a freely smiling face
would crumble in white sweat: he also wanted his victim,
after his return from the long journey of his suffering, to
love him. In the tropical light of insanity the ghosts of this
cellar bar could communicate only in the nonsense syl-
lables of sexual violence. There were those who broke into
pieces for their God and gushed forth pity for their tormentors. The torturer seeks two kinds of men: those who
throw themselves at his mercy, and those from whom, in
return for torture, he will ask forgiveness. Even after the
severance of all human ties, the victim must know that the
tormentor, too, has a drop of that otherworldly fuel that he
is trying to dry up in his prisoner. Toward dawn, when they
were both on the floor grunting from exhaustion, simple,
human dialogues were born. Perhaps this was the secret
that those who stayed in this cellar did not want to reveal,
even those who had the strength to abandon their old
selves and fly over their bodies the way a swallow flies over
a burning house, high in the sky, where even the smoke
can't reach.

They would rather tell stories about the onetime chief of
this tribunal that has now been reconverted into a cellar

bar. He liked to visit kindergartens and play the violin for the children. He watched quietly in the corner and almost never interfered with his henchmen; only in critical moments did he lean forward with intense curiosity, chewing all the while the tip of his pipe. When his turn finally came, his two favorite assistants carried him downstairs. The noiseless, ironic man hung on to every bar of the railing. He screamed and fought and begged the subordinates he met on the stairs to save him. Nobody made as much noise as he when they bound him and laid him out on the cold, sawdust-covered concrete floor amid the machinery of his own resourcefulness and discarded cigarette butts. Five of his men, and a stranger, stood over him and trained the floodlights on him, and waved sticks in the air, and cranked the pulleys, and turned on the dental drills, and poured acid from one bottle into the other. He had never seen such intense curiosity on the faces of his men. They watched him as he wailed louder than anyone before him in that cellar, but did not touch him. He must also have been cunning enough to know that by grabbing at their boots, by crying and messing in his pants, he was pleasing them: his men did want to see just that. They never touched him, but when the stranger gave the signal, the five of them fired into their chief's body without asking a single question.

At half past three in the morning, when others die, I put on a black shirt and coat. I have to leave. I close the door very quietly behind me, and flee my shadow on the glistening snow. I hear every snowflake fall, the clink of their tiny skeletons makes me shudder. Without your feet, these polished shoes seem pointless; I picture you in all the coats put out in shopwindows. I see a great black hearse, a great white sheepskin, and your green little body on a stretcher. I walk past hoary snapshots: I relive your death. I relished the Sundays of your body, and now I lower the eyelids of December. The semantic struggle between *I* and *you* cannot come to an end. I survive in your pulse, revoke your heart failure, and complicate your histories—you died be-

fore I could adjust to your silence. I do not feel at home anywhere; every belly grows cold under me. I go from woman to woman, from mother to daughter. Who is going to take me in on this night of abandonment? I can't apprehend the shiver of my bones; I need you to exist; I must return to your lap. I am surrounded by the dripstones of a historical slaughterhouse, and only you could lead me back to the warm stable of identity. If I could utter the word *you*, I wouldn't seem so insipid.

Stones and steps exude peace. I remain alone with my body; I can no longer help you. I see black urine on white snow, and a peeping poster-child. Whom are these surgical knives waiting for; who is looking through glasses darkly? I am lost in the error of a great smile; I immerse myself in the milk of the world, soak up absence with a piece of bread, and put it into my mouth: now I can resume my historical blunders. I have with me an entire traveling circus, and though I am thirsty, I can't stop anywhere, for I am afraid they will notice my menagerie. I got a taste of existence; more than this I cannot ask for. Blond gods hang upside down in a lamp shop; pipe-smoking murderers signal to one another from every doorstep; I catch a glimpse of a raised billiard cue, a lucky hole: three wise men play pool with my bone balls. I bury myself in narrow streets; I carry enough corpses to fill a trench. I walk from one world war into another, and shrouded windows drop dirty excuses in front of my feet. I ought to know where I am: I stumble on embarrassing fornicators; their flesh watches their bones; attention regards itself. This red scarf is now the entire city; I can penetrate it, I can take upon myself its favorite or horrible vicissitudes. Another challenge: I put my head on a tree, and reach for the roots through its trunk; but after much strain, I end up where I started from. The church steeple bends over ever so quietly; under the roof of my mouth, a staircase collapses, I am slashed by voiceless speech, corridors open behind my back, I hear the shriek of a headless rooster. Amid so much rubble, admonitions penetrate my vitals; yet I remain a disabled and deteriorating vehicle. I hear someone saying he has to urinate. Who is unbuttoning my pants before the brick wall of shame? Whose genitals are these, and whose words, which follow me and label things? Here I stand, afraid I will forget even my name. Cars pass and won't turn off their high beams. Under the iconostasis of windows, a dog is pulled on a leash; it tries hard to lift its hind legs, but the tug on its collar is too strong. An old lady with thighs as thick as milestones approaches: she collects rags in wheelbarrows and tumbrels, and now wants to pick me up, too. In the redundant circle of streets, I try to break loose from my own self, and from falling plaster, and posters sticking out their tongues in the wind. I hear stray shots; the nape of my neck feels heavy. In the gleam of moon-deserts, in the halo of a single gas flame, I run after you. I cover vast distances, but as the retaining walls of consciousness quietly cave in, I end up in the same cruel square, where dough-fleshed, pudgy creatures run about giggling and howling.

I can feel your shivers, your age; we shared our youth and our senility. I pursue you; I feed on your memory. I would send you trees, gods, words. Only if dictionaries caved in would we be separated by a rubble of speech. But on this terrifying tightrope-existence, we are still responsible for each other. I eat with your mouth, breathe with your lungs, shut my eyes with your lids—and feel uncertain in your belly. Your flesh rots, but you won't allow anyone to see it. I blame you because for a moment you peer at me with my mother's eyes: I am afraid you can manage without me. You were here once; I used you for a blanket; in you a single moment lasted for hours. Now I look for you in store signs, in walls, and can't find you even in the blind alleys of memory. The shadow play of two kindred spirits fills my mind with lies; I am tired of lugging myself after you. I proceed on the suspension bridge of my cough to the other side of the street; you can meet me, your invisible flesh can be a summer in this heavy snowfall. How many fields of ice can separate two people, how many thorny twigs must I break off before reaching your body, how many times must I draw myself aside like a curtain? You disappeared early; you didn't want to be present in the square where I am surrounded by my friends, the agents of disclosures, who cover me silently with stones and dirt. Words are lime-covered rags, my peat-filled mouth caves in; all I know is that you were here. You are absent-minded, like a candle flame with a finger passing through it. Take a look at the horse that left its harness behind and drags around its dried-up testicles on this square of homelessness. Do help me for once; I don't enjoy crouching helplessly; perhaps you shall pull me out from under the square's pavement, and take me away from this cluster of light. We met at the lit-up station too late, we missed our connection, and you took with you only my unhappy, worn-out words.

I stand on this icy square and would like to leave the city behind as morning leaves night behind. On the church square of collective presence I am besieged by questions. I live the lies of motion as I bite into a piece of bread. Someone lets go the assassin of surprise, and suspends the evil teleology that interconnects stair, heel, teeth, and bread. Who stands behind the smashed mirrors? Who left for an unknown destination, who walks on the pavement, who is being addressed, who speaks? Whom must I watch and keep from being run over? Who drops his guard and survives dangerous moments; who is the one who sees himself in others; whom must I see to see You? Deceiving each other, giving testimony against each other—what would we be doing now? The sun is out; we smile pleasantly and are ready to introduce ourselves. We are the oft-deceived homeless, who are asked to move on, to complete the journey imposed on us, and finally to return to this suspicious-looking church square. We hold a candle in our hand; we are ourselves a reflection of the candle. I drag myself from palm to palm, from square to square, and from question to question.

Our Father was also asked to join us tonight, but He is nowhere in sight. Even if He were here, He would just look at us helplessly—a question among many other questions. Only the hypocrites pretend to be mingling; catatonic silence can also be a spectacle. The cheats insinuate themselves into the ground.

At dawn I thought it was impossible; now I know it is possible. I stand before your church in the square, and would like to receive you as a guest in my mind's domain. I need you, for you are the promise inherent in every street; I could address you in each of them. But you didn't send for me, didn't call me. I will not sweeten my breath with excuses; I will not bear grudges. After all, my history is your history, you are the helpless victim of my knowledge, my greatest abstraction; we keep constructing and killing each other. Still, I vie for your love, for your being; as I cling to you, our thoughts begin to live. I don't like sugary church sermons; they are out to persuade, and pronounce self-denial freedom. I am interested in everything said about you, but am bored if it's said from a pulpit. Sermons cannot surprise; statements about what is permitted and what is not leave no room for thought, a speech from a pulpit imprisons you in chattering silence. I often doubt you, though I need you; I am not horrified by the inevitability of my heresies, though I cannot reconcile them with my earnest goals. I need you to connect me with my loved ones during hours of need, during wedding nights, in isolation wards, in transcendent moments. We can call each other on a direct line, and that reassures me. When I realize that everyone who encourages me to be a traitor is sane and only I am crazy, I have a good laugh with you, emperor of lunatics. Holding my son's hand, I can feel the warmth of every boy's hand. Perhaps it's your doing that my aged, incontinent relative doesn't disgust me; while cleaning his behind, I am cleansing myself. In your presence, even on crowded streetcars, I am not praying for the deliverance of the next second. By paying attention only to you, I find my city surprisingly cozy; every morning I think it is my birthday. I do not think my fellow travelers either superfluous or indispensable; I look for reflections of my own fate in every living organism. I like my meager, puny race, and am ready to believe that there are infinitely greater minds than my own. Still, they are all my relatives, struggling to master their surroundings. They are your relatives, too, and share the tension of the universe even as they are dying. I like the comedy of your multifaceted self; I need an irresponsible mind to define you. If you are good, there exists a devil whom you can't always control; if you are everything, you contain that devil, and you can't always control yourself. If I see you as my friend, you begin to resemble me too much: you are a reformist intellectual in opposition to the existing order. You have neither money nor weapons; no one really pays any attention to you. I ask in vain for your help. If you are good, then let's be objective and admit that I don't even live in your city; you don't even have a city, and no matter how much you might resist the thought, an earthquake is imminent; we are on the verge of collapse, the eerie, empty silence fences us in. If you are not the all-knowing boss, you, too, will lament the breakup of star clusters, feel the sting of coincidence, and have trouble conceiving of total destruction. But if you *are* the all-powerful theater-director, you size me up somewhat ironically. Though you manage your stage well, I begin to suspect you, and doubt your claim that self-awareness that perceives its limits can desire its own perpetuation. The inquisitor and heretic merge in you when you encourage me to go on, and you look around guiltily when you approve of my failures. Why, then, should I, a dot in the infinity of ignorance, who have a picture of the builder in front of me when I see a building, team up with you? At most we can become accomplices. If you are the indivisible Mother, who is reborn in eternal solitude, who is not confronted by anyone and encompasses all your future goals; if you are one who can't judge the world because you are everything— then you are nothing, and astronomy is closer to you than earthly love. I can stand before you, surprised and hostile; the cleverer I am the more superfluous I become—a hollow name instead of a meaningful one. I don't need you just so I can praise you while admiring the structure of the solar system or of a worm. If you weren't good and evil in one, I would have to invent someone in your stead with whom I could conspire against the tedious order of things.

I don't want to cut myself off from the city. Someone I know is walking across the square, and he is as much my relative as I am his; our sameness is uncanny. Three hundred thousand people constitute one curriculum; we are tenants in a square furnished by the centuries—legendary heroes from the book of omissions, princes joining hands in a spring procession in the courtyard of treacherous insanity. If we were to link together our inhabitants' consciousness, the coal of the dead, the peat of the living would burn in the powerhouse of a single archetype. If with every helpless utterance I could draw sustenance from the subterranean heat of cultures; if, unable to become God, I could at least avoid being as lonely as the wretches kneeling in front of altar rails; if I could stretch my experiences until they began to resemble others'—then, sitting in the electric chair of the city's consciousness, could I command the faith that is a city builder's ultimate undoing? I huddle in the shell-bottom of my sunken city; I shiver in the womb of a self-supporting community, which belligerent and gallant ambition would forever like to impregnate. I believe my presence here is an accident; my absent-minded progress on a tiny planet is utterly devoid of significance. My protracted and imperfect death, which can turn into a perfect one any second, is not a parable, not a horror story, not even a dull inside view of hell. I am not interested in forestalling my appointed time; it will not be any more pleasant to chat on stone steps or read under the plane trees next year than it is this year. The sun is out; it is so easy to love others as they cross my field of vision: their profile is mine. I am both viewer and actor; I banish the word *mine*, and when told I cannot judge what is beyond me, I say we are all good judges; neither God nor what we call history is any better than man. A wounded go-getter finally left me on the wet stone floor of a windowless cell. He would have lifted me out of time and made sure I was as different from him as a swimmer is from the water he is in, but not different enough to make me fight the current. Stuck in the cage of my body and my days, I want to get rid of this neighbor, who is noisy but does little. Whatever is outside of him is his enemy; and, while guarding his home with the alertness of an exorcist, he populates it with demons. I choose to practice the eroticism of immobility: raise your hand, I whisper, and bless this city mercilessly, all of it, as it is.

As cars find their way in the square even with their head-lights turned off, or come to a halt, disperse, pile up again, and ultimately make the right turn; as singing soldiers and tied-down cattle find their trucks, prisoners their corridors, corpses their hearses, bakery rolls their wire baskets—so does everything find its proper place in the universal scheme of things. The fingers of infants and old men touch, revolving entrance and exit doors complement each other, the dead don't stay on earth, lovers ultimately meet, insults reach their addressees, soldiers their barracks, scientists their conferences, the occupants of death row, the stone prison yard. Social position and sexual lure keep fluctuating according to secret and ever-changing rates on the invisible market of youth and intelligence. Every quirk falls into place, on nudist sundecks, in the confession booths, in a mini-theater, on the dissecting table. At times like these I am convinced that existence is not a scandal, that I or another, success or failure, is really the same; that this city is able to endure the wastefulness of people and things, that a pair of golden legs in red panties is such a timeless treasure to the one looking at it, touching it, or owning it, that it cannot be erased even if she is run over by a streetcar, even if a whole new forest of legs is planted on the pavement the next day; that stupidity and fear cannot corrupt the sweetness of existence, that the misery of our repetitions, and the pain in our tender organs, eventually dissolve under the sun, that in the vast traffic of animate and inanimate things there is no cause for either hope or despair, for there is only that light over the city, the race of day and night, the enormous dazzle of time, the permissive curves of space, and our slow progress toward death, which, even if it keeps us waiting a while longer and lets us open our eyes a few more times, is ultimately our friend.

I don't want to forget that this city, whose shame I know so well, also belongs to those who walked up to marching columns being led away and offered them bread; who didn't allow the victims' names to be scratched off registries, who called murderers and friends by their true names. It is also the city of resistance, the city that tamed hostile governors and made possible mental readjustments and the reassessment of sanctified privileges. It is the city of belated appreciation, and of people who make sense out of moronic tasks and begin work on freedom by first demolishing their own obsessions. I don't want to look glassy-eyed at loved ones crushed to a red pulp, or at prisoners who shovel next to rifle-carrying guards, or at wheezing old men forced to rest on every bench, or at a child crying because of senseless regulations. I don't want to stare at people who swallow gas out of fear, who are astonished at being stabbed in the back. I don't want to gape at the prayer of hatred in front of multistory statues of dictators, at the parodies of need in shopwindows, at traps on writing desks set for itself by the mind, at mechanics' slow suicide behind heavy, slowly turning wheels, at drawn shutters behind which there are two people of whom only one can ask questions, at chained prisoners marching through endless corridors, at the senile smiles of geniuses as they bend over the plate of exhaustion and with blind hands grope for bits of food; at women huddling at the foot of a bed, being hit on the stomach by miserable men, at interrogations remaining in manuscript, at plans marooned in words, embraces withered by the shiver of anxiety, insults floating forever in the hall of memory, at retired murderers' dentures standing between their memoirs and the morning cup of coffee. I reject the gesture of benediction as inane surrender. This city is my crippled charge: I simply couldn't stay in the cage where my mother bore her litter.

The copper strips of the departing summer edge through the slats of my shutter, slice up my face, and stretch out on my bed. I hear the horn of a hydrofoil; my furniture soaks in honey, and my room swings into fall and winter on the merry-go-round of the seasons. I think of New Year's Eve: a paper trumpet blasts in my ear, a devil's tongue jumps into my mouth, a happy rooster puts his arm around me. We can sit on streetcar tracks, pin mistletoe on the reluctant traffic-cop, and make noise with officially licensed rattles in underground arcades. Drunks crouch on equestrian statues and in tar-smelling urinals; floodlights are turned on, frozen feet skate on the cobblestones of the main square: a band steps out on a balcony. Make way for the hermaphrodite guitar, the guffawing, silver-tailed saxophones, the heaven-beseeching trombones, the savage drum; explode the night with sounds. Wearing a fringed leather jacket and a gold headband, the bandleader takes up his position. He holds the microphone to his mouth, tosses back his hair, and leads the swelling ecstasy. Sawing up the frozen layers of night, he outbellows pneumatic drills and the clatter of iron doors. Roller-shutters break, signposts topple, newspapers burn, barracks doors are flung open, and in the darkened night the electric news-flashes of surprises are switched on. Tonight do not fear police lines, upholstered doors, remote-control detectors; do not fear beltless pants, laceless shoes, rubber tubes placed in nostrils —do not fear fear. Tonight doors aren't locked, and you can knock over your tray in the mess hall. No one stands behind the floodlights in the guard tower, and you can make it to the next corner without valid traveling papers. Doors have knobs on both sides, and you can ask any question, for tonight all statements need proof and no decisions are made in secret. You can rehearse your utopias tonight and be intimate with the classics—you can just *be* tonight for the sake of being. Your hair is white from the powder of fireworks, your shoulder is wet from fresh snow, you perspire from all the shouting: put on your coat, my son. Don't bother telling me I am right; we can't absolve each other of our errors. There are many floors in the staircase of love, including the floor of violence. The hungry have no time for scruples; but if you have enough food, have dignity as well. You are impatient, and would remain so even if you were at the top. Try to avoid getting there—you need too many accomplices for that. My poor old child, while you are trying to lower yourself, they keep rising in you. When phrases like "the sun is out," or "the wind blows," become loaded statements, do not try to be objective; when the mind turns out pretexts, let the foolish be smart. On your way up on that stairway of love, you may get into trouble. I would fortify you with tried and true arguments, and help you stand above me in the cemetery; but I would gladly miss the moment of your disillusionment, when boredom triumphs over discernment. Come what may, my son, I stand behind you. My room turns back to summer again: I keep clutching the ring of the merry-go-round, a player piano plays, we fly past courtyards, attic windows, and cemeteries. An errant hit-song is saying farewell to red-mouthed photographs glued to tombstones.

Blow your horn at pock-marked brick walls, at giggling cats and peeping, fat faces in shopwindows; at the white-stoned City Hall that turned black in this grim neighbor-hood, at windows in which meat is stored in blood-soaked wrapping paper, at a Central European square that is mentioned in histories of architecture, at heroes held in national reverence, at the green bronze mantle of the poet, from which the rain quietly rinses ossified bird-droppings, and under which we are lulled to sleep by familiar speeches. Blow your horn at the statue of the poet, because what else remains of the man's restless endeavors, of his life's work? And blow your horn at the statue of the general who sits on his horse in a posture of command, his face radiant with determination. He reins in his fighter horse, which is balanced by a tail embedded in massive stones. The steed will go on raising itself amid the blast of trum-pets, above the geometrically flawless carpet of white-clothed gymnasts and white-gloved cadets. And blow your horn into the face of fear; mock the impossible with a fiendish grimace, jump over metaphysical vomit-puddles. A bloody handkerchief lies on the ground: find your stabbed friend, follow the path of spilled blood. This celebration unites the entire city; we reword the rules of the night, ban the rancid warnings of seriousness, and toss our fur hats on the ground. We are brave because we blow our horns in unison, brandish our triumphant instruments, and hear the echo of your laughter. Unbutton your coat, let the snow fall on your bare chest; look up and take in the winter's night with the astonished gaze of a calf.

You must live for the holiday; tonight boredom is a capital offense. Destroy the silent night, reclaim the world with joy, banish routine; if you waste this hour, tomorrow will not back you up. A crazy year is over; what have you done all this time? Where are the circled dates on your calendar? It is up to you to pry open locked minutes, to tremble with the stage fright of freedom, to look at horrible window displays in utter bafflement. You sit in each other's silence; you think you know all there is to know about the other person, but that voiceless explosion with which the soul cuts loose from its mooring and becomes a white arrow in the sky, you dare mention only with a hesitant smile. Humiliate yourself; make your face burn more intensely than a riverbank on the morning of the longest day of the year. Let this face be your gift to yourself—live, don't snuff out your senses. Tomorrow you may hang yourself; or you may emigrate from your passport picture into an equatorial-polar denial of that excessively narrow and moderate zone where you have been fretting up to now. Keep walking until you clutch a fence post and slowly sink on your knees; or remain immobile until unclasping your hands will seem like a miracle. You are terrified; they can still touch you and tell you things you do not dare hear. Defy them all and say the word that takes your breath away; daub your face, your house, your world with the images of your terror, carve your ideas on tree trunks, your freedom on blocks of ice. Don't build new wings for your prisons, don't burn live offerings before the false gods of resignation; instead, enrich your moments in the quick oven of existence, let its light penetrate your lunar nerves. No reward or recognition can make you become your own friend; no one can surpass you in your thirst for defeat. Do not be modest, drink to every life in this city that you made yours. Your technique was childish, your self-justifications inadequate, your achievements pathetic. But save, save what you can; your misfortunes are not sewed under your skin—this celebration is fast becoming a revolution. Stop bartering and manipulating; stop brooding over your troubles; say no lovingly to your inquisitors; stretch out on the body of time, and in the midst of erupting seconds, air your room, change your bed sheets, listen to the bells, and say your cruel goodbyes.

We taste one another's drinks and devour one another in the main square. Everything celebrates everything else; our strength will surely hold out for another year. Now you can summon your fugitive friend; let him retrace his dive back to a seventh-floor window, and let the guardian of your loyalty, the adventurous prince of your irreligious religion, disappear from his underground confessional. You can wait for him in the square of interrogations, and watch together a wild-eyed man oozing out of the ground in a lambskin coat and high boots. He saws the air with hands clasped for prayer and, with a cowbell jangling around his neck, rushes after gold-helmeted boys whose necks are slenderer than the wine flask he offers to everyone. Amid crushed trumpets he embraces a sooty gypsy: he promises him City Hall, not just a mud house. He tosses back his hair, and his nightmares, and begins to shriek on a clarinet. He gives a four-leaf clover to an old woman who is backing out of the yellow cone of a street light; in a moment of compassion, he lifts her high above the crowd. Between pairs of eyes focused on one another, he recognizes forest fires of hate, but he can't say a thing to his enemies, must avoid them and hurry on to the next attraction. A dancer is poised on a board placed on a cylinder. There is a silver sash in the black cleft of her buttocks and horizontal eights around her eyes. (Yes, we shall all meet in infinity.) Midnight is here: trumpets screech, we plant kisses on one another's ear lobes, couples flee putrid TV screens, the gestures of strain flood the street, everyone offers the square some foolish feat. In underground urinals, shifty onanists eye one another; couples with nailed-down faces shake the saliva out of their red paper horns and blow on them with growing desperation; a cripple kicks aside a broken wine bottle and taps on the pavement with his crutch; we would all like to do something very special tonight but don't know what.

Grab a zither, make a tour of the town, drift down to the main square on the beaten track of celebration, appear on the stage of tests and disruptions, where your murderers and victims fight it out to the bitter end. Tonight you will feel what others felt before you; generations of people will join you—everyone who had a part in the drama of your evolution. The square closes shut between the cathedral and the hotel: it takes a century to cover the distance between a tree and a lamppost. Universities of thought and matter collapse and rise again; you nail yourself under the shadow and light and mildew of this square of recognition. Don't leave; you are in the right place; wait for the messages. Here come a white reindeer and a cat-faced mailman. Tonight even your horrified eyeball is a spy; the labyrinths of bewitchment are blocked, and the police chief of your skull refashions your defenses in his own image. You are the only spectator on stage; if you stand up, rag-glass-platinum draperies begin to rustle. Cynical orators and sweaty envoys ham it up just for you; threadbare actors and sneaky moralists keep stumbling before you—you don't know whether to stab them or kiss them. Every face hurts and pleases on this square of animal compassion. There is only one that angers you: worms swarm on his dark tongue and he wants to lick you. Another looks like a village graveyard with wooden markers; his hand, as he gives you light, is a triptych in front of your empty face. The markings fall out of your calendar of deeds; a crooked fetus, you swim backward in a golden lake, toward airless, fat cells, and then shoot yourself back into the square, where you are still a spectator. If you pay attention, your fellow citizens reveal themselves like posters on a billboard. You laugh at over-cautious allusions, humorous surprises, even though you yourself are the director of the passion play of experience and intelligence on this square. You hesitate: are you walking on a stage, or is the stage in you? It is tiring to carry an entire city around your neck, to pick up an entire inert world like a sheaf of messages. But you no longer want to decipher the symbols of continuity on this insensate square. If you give accident its freedom, you are the one to whom, in whom, everything happens. Slowly but surely, you, too, are becoming a loud, senseless windbag, a black-brained ram. You grapple with shadows, are ready to help others, and can never sit still long enough to listen to your own heartbeat. When you hear the drums roll, you can't come to terms with your eyes and settle down in the valley of vision. You look for complex moves to accompany the simplest truths. Flotsam of existence: you want to be its sun. You are not willing to admit that suffering is the main theme of the play enacted on this square; nor are you ready to defy that suffering with a richer anguish of your own. You will not allow your life to creep behind you. You would like to be outside, but we are all in here. You keep asking questions, don't recognize people from their smiles, and argue even with those you have already killed in your heart.

A red shirt is unbuttoned on a flesh-colored mannequin;

glass bells tinkle on pine-tree branches; a cotton-bearded coconut's pointy silver hat tilts sideways; a drunken child huddles in a top hat—his eyes, as he looks through his cotton candy, order his enemies to board a white ship, and on the open seas the ship sinks along with its cargo. Under sparkling light-bulb-fruits, a girl with hair that reaches down to the hem of her fur coat slurps her third raw egg. Lovers busy biting each other's lips hover around her, black-faced wayfarers of the night blow trumpets in her ear; a leather-coated agent of revelations, relaxing his grip on his night stick, drifts toward her; a youth, his face white from masturbation, kneels down before her, and glides his finger-tips down her legs: he would like to devour her like a giant banana. Quietly cruising taxi drivers in devil masks stop at her side for a moment, a drunk goes up to her and demands to know: Why am I Paul and not Peter? But neither of them can solve the mystery. A gypsy woman who usually dozes behind her flowers and chestnuts offers the girl a lucky horseshoe, along with cat and bear masks; a blind man clutches her arm with a deceptively dreamy smile: until now he has been guessing the flavor of homes in which Christmas building-blocks construct themselves and electric trains clatter across frontiers. A curly-bearded, greasy Ethiopian, who is trying to wring a children's song out of his single-tone flute, now whirls around the girl with a triple-flamed torch; a woman who will not laugh drags her two children to see him, and then runs back to her apartment, where she didn't light the fire because the one for whom she would have loved to do it left her. This is a night of intermingling; the city is a single happening. The yolk of a raw egg trickles down the girl's finger, and hides the golden marks of suicide on her palm.

Everything will come to pass during this quiet liberation, everyone will be a host on the main square: you can talk to yourself, you know more than what you are. You toll the

bell for the living, dart across town, ice-skate at the head of
your armies, summon the silent prisoners who look through
the windows of the past, blow up the underground poison
mines of anxiety, throw the spiked apples of encourage-
ment into strange homes, and drop ten precisely formu-
lated questions into mailboxes. You lean over a dying man
who only moves his eyes and tell him: yes, yes; you warm
the cold feet of an old woman who stares at the light of a
candle; you give a cup of soup to a worker who fell silent
eight days ago and refused to eat; you invite a handicapped
champion runner to the victory platform; you help a cowardly executioner mount a red horse on a merry-go-round.
You peel threats off an oil-brown wall and replace them
with a single, unforgettable sentence. You look in a mirror
and find the person you have long sought. With her you
stream over granite blocks polished smooth by time. Pressing your forehead against hers, you pass on your palsied
memories. While holding her hand on a bench, you can't
hear protest songs or explanations of the probability theory: in the naked silence, two bellies, two world views
touch. The razor blade of surrender has so far eluded her
face, disgust has not yet pulled down its shutters on dialogue: things could still happen. Under the shower each
morning a community recommences its history—a community whose present condition even God Himself couldn't
define, and whose hateful and sweet images are petrified in
time. You lift the main square of your city over your head,
and touch the face of a woman in it; in the special-events
calendar of your mind, this gesture remains a holiday. Bird-
of-paradise words escape unnoticed from her mouth; the
molehills of consciousness erupt around her shoes; slender,
hairy things and silvered statues emerge from the ground.
In your imploring fingers you feel the power of pain; in
her eye sockets matriarchs watch. She places the crown of
emperor-beggars on your head, removes herself from the

swaddling clothes of forgetfulness, and you both find yourselves sitting on the ivy-clad dead. Do not panic, your resting foot will receive satisfaction for every false step; it's her shirt but you unbutton your own nakedness, not even a pickax can pierce your narrow chest. You place her stone-bright, mineral hand on your head, and she bids you to exist.

You can at last immerse yourself in the beatified crowd; you can brandish your noisemakers. This day makes all the others tolerable; we will go on listening to respectable grunts for another year, but right now we clamor for the tail of a pig. Dazed vandals are on the march, and pulpy faces flaunt their own strangeness. An old man elbows his way through the crowd; he'll be gone by spring, but now his clown hat and two mateless vampire-teeth shake as he laughs. The crowd surges; wives don't belong to husbands and husbands are without wives. When you are lost in one vast family it is easy to scream; all songs can be sung now, a shepherd's air blends in with a Gregorian chant. Snow covers the lanterns: go on vomiting in a paper hat, winter's troubled sleep and prayers to an anarchist butcher on herring-smelling sheets are yet to come. They stick a microphone in your hand: you expect to stay alive in the new year. You lean on the egg-munching girl, who attached a car horn to her trumpet; snow falls in her mouth, she laughs and kisses herself and, swaying her head, says: Suck my blood. Somebody gives her a drum; she holds it between her knees and squats and leaps as she beats it. A band of people with mocking, clumsy gestures murmur behind her; a fat ghost, a plumed furnace, yellow eyes, hawk nose: a bird-bodied figure in shirt sleeves cuts through the crowd. Gap-toothed revelers throw one another in the air, women in fur coats and bastionlike hairdos enjoy a piggyback ride on one another's shoulders, the party is in full swing, everyone loves everyone else, we form a never-to-bedissolved alliance, even the word will come to us, which will impart meaning to our wild whinnying, something may yet grow at the foot of the baroque palaces, elevated now to office buildings. Dive onto the dance floor, laugh divinely, take your place in the fast-moving circle, black-mouthed dancers: let's do outrageous steps, let's invade the ramparts, the pulpits, the reviewing stands, let's occupy all the empty spaces. The trumpet-chimneys of cars bellow away, couples wave kerchief-flags and trot off to side streets; the square toasts itself, now you, too, are important, you who wave your hand and stamp your foot only when no one is around, everyone greets everyone else, strangers fall ecstatically on one another's necks, flares whiz by and illuminate the sky, no one strikes his neighbor, this night is the answer to our national silence. A red strip moves across the electric news-banner, but when it's light again, broken glass, mangled noisemakers, and masks limp before the giant sweeper. It was only a bit of tomfoolery, a picnic in the snow, a revolution of trumpets and horns. On the frosty window of a crowded streetcar a passenger writes the date of the new year, and then draws a line through it, crosswise.